Emma

A Hollywood novel
by Stacey Broadbent

Published by Stacey Broadbent, Ashburton, NZ
Copyright 2019 © Stacey Broadbent

Proofreading by Spell Bound
Cover image from Deposit Photos
Cover Design by Stacey Broadbent
Font: Open Dyslexic

ISBN: 978-0-473-47310-5
         978-0-473-47311-2
         978-0-473-47312-9
         978-0-473-47313-6
         979-8-839-30422-2
         978-1-0670111-3-0 (Dyslexia friendly)

Emma

A Hollywood novel
by Stacey Broadbent

Contents

Author's note

The main character in this book is from New Zealand, so some NZ slang terms have been used. These are not errors, it's just the way we speak over here.

Dedicated to

The Ashburton Writers' Group, for taking me out of my comfort zone and challenging me to write to a different topic each month. This started out as an assignment and took on a life of its own!

Chapter one

"Oomph." I trip over my own feet as I make my way up the red carpet in a gown they promised would suck in my wobbly bits but remain comfortable. They lied. The mermaid style dress clings to every curve of my body, accentuating my round ass and showing off every little dimple. Of course, I only noticed this after I'd bought it and removed the tags. That'll teach me for downing a bottle of chardonnay before going frock shopping.

"Emma! This way!" the paparazzi call out my name and I go through the motions of posing for photos, all the while wishing I had a drink in my hand. If only I'd had the forethought to bring some of those little bottles of spirits that fit perfectly in your purse. Oh wait! That's right, I did. With nimble fingers, I make quick work of the zip on my purse and surreptitiously pull out a mini bottle of Smirnoff. Palming it, I make my way along the carpet, desperately seeking a bathroom where I can sneak a drink away from prying eyes. You never can be too careful when the paparazzi are out in full force.

I don't make it very far before I'm ushered through to the ballroom where tables are laden with champagne and caviar. A grin spreads across my face as I tuck my mini bottle back inside my purse for later and make my way to table number twelve.

I find the seat with my name on it and pour myself a hefty glass of bubbles while I poke through the goodie bag they've left me. I'd heard word of how amazing these things are, and man, were they right! A night in Rhode Island, a day spa voucher, a fancy candle, makeup from various sponsors, and my personal favorite, a case of champagne to be delivered to my door. What more could a girl want?

The room slowly fills as I drink my way through another bottle of champers, making small talk with the rest of the table. My accent always throws them, and I have to remind myself to talk slower, so people can understand me. When I'm on the job it's not an issue as I've been with a dialect coach for the past two years, but after a few too many drinks, the kiwi accent comes out thick and strong.

The lights dim and music blasts through the room as Jimmy Fallon takes to the stage. It's been a dream of mine to meet him, and when I found out he'd be hosting tonight, I nearly peed my pants. I may be up for an award, but that doesn't mean I can't still fangirl over Jimmy. In fact, there are a lot of people here tonight that I never in my wildest dreams imagined I'd get the chance to meet. And here I am, the little kiwi gal from nowheresville, pretending I'm one of them. It's surreal, to say the least.

After an hour or two of smiling and clapping, I realize it's finally time; they're announcing my category. This is it! My big moment! It's my first award show and I'm up for one of the most prestigious awards; best actress. Who'd have thought? Little ol' me from New Zealand hobnobbing with the best. The competition is fierce too. I'm up against some of Hollywood's finest; Julia Roberts, Charlize Theron, Scarlett Johansen and Emma Stone.

I suck in a breath and plaster a smile on my face as the camera lands on me while they announce my name and the movie I'm nominated for.

The room goes quiet as they rip the envelope open. I can barely breathe. My heart pounds in my chest, and I quickly down another glass of bubbles in nervous anticipation. I've lost count how many I've had now.

"And the winner is..."

Did they just say what I think they said?

My ears ring and tears spring to my eyes as I hear the uttering of my name from their lips. I practise my surprised face; a hand to my chest as I nod at those around my table. Standing, I make my way through the crowd and up to the stage. The presenter, some young hotshot who rose to fame on Nickelodeon, I forget his name, is reluctant to hand over my prized award, but I wrench it from his hands, holding it close to my heart as I make my way to the mic on wobbly legs.

Perhaps I shouldn't have had so much champagne.

"Wow. I can't believe this is actually happening," I start. To my left, the presenters whisper to each other but I try my best to ignore them. They won't ruin my moment. I've worked too hard and too long for this. I glance to the shiny gold man in my hands, feeling fresh tears pooling in my eyes. "I'd like to thank—"

I'm cut off by a hand on my shoulder. A man dressed in black stands just behind me, motioning for me to join him. I shrug him off. "Do you mind? I'm kind of in the middle of something." I quirk an eyebrow at him before turning back to the crowd, muttering, "Some people," under my breath.

"Ah, there seems to have been a misunderstanding." The presenter has squeezed into the gap between me and the mic and is addressing the audience. More men dressed in black appear at the side of the stage and I frown in confusion. "The winner was Emma Stone, not Emma Jones."

I shake my head.

No, that's not right. My name is Emma Jones.

I glance around the room and see Emma standing off to the side with an apologetic look on her face while the audience titters amongst themselves. Through my drink-addled haze, I can just make out their pitying looks and hear their whispered remarks.

"Is she drunk?"

"Isn't that the New Zealand actress?"

"She actually thought she won? How embarrassing."

I look back to the man in my hands, gently caressing a finger down the length as I shut out the harshness of their words. They don't know what they're talking about. They called *my* name out. They did. I'm almost ninety percent sure of it.

A little voice whispers in my head, "They can't take this away from me. Possession is nine tenths of the law. They called my name."

My eyes flick up to the presenter and I take a step forward as if I'm going to hand it over, but instead I hoist my skirt and dart down the stairs and back through the crowd, my trophy held high above my head. "I'll never part with it!" I cry out, fighting my way through the throngs of people on the floor. "You'll have to wrestle it from my cold, dead body before I let you take it!"

I don't really have a plan and that becomes abundantly obvious when I chance a glance at the door I'd come through only a few hours earlier. Those damn men in black are everywhere, surrounding me. They block the exits and I can hear their thundering steps coming up from behind. I stop, brandishing my statue like a sword as I turn in a frenzied circle, my eyes darting between each of them.

A thick arm wraps around my waist from behind and I'm lifted into the air, my legs and arms flailing about until, in slow motion, my little gold man flies from my hand and bounces across the floor. The fight leaves me as I crumple to the ground in a sobbing mess. I'm hauled to my feet and led out to the foyer where I'm promptly plonked on the nearest bench. The men in black straighten their suits, turn on their heels and stride back through the door, and I hear the distinct sound of a lock being snicked.

I stare at the door, silently willing it to open, for someone to apologize and tell me it was all a misunderstanding, but deep down, I know it's not going to happen. My first awards show, and I make a fool of myself in front of so many actors I admire, not to mention the millions of viewers who will no doubt be calling me a crazy drunk. I can see it now, my name splashed across the tabloids, and not in a good way.

God, I need a drink.

My head snaps up as I realize I've left the goodie bag behind, complete with the details on how to claim my case of champagne.

Damn it!

With an almighty sigh, I pull myself up to stand, instantly thrown off balance by a missing heel. It must've fallen off in my scuffle with the men in black. *Could this night get any worse?*

I sniff and wipe my eyes, slowly hobbling to the curb to call a cab.

Chapter two

"Noooo!" I scream as I jolt awake, clutching my pillow for dear life. My bedsheets are strewn every which way, and my silk negligee is twisted around my body like some sort of Houdini escape suit. I pant, the remnants of my dream still clinging desperately to my subconscious. Rolling to my side, a groan slips from my lips as I slowly peel my eyes open. My head pounds as the sunlight hits my retinas through the curtains I'd neglected to close before passing out last night, and I'm reminded of the twinkling lights of the awards show. The camera flashes, the glitz and glamor of the fantastical light show on display in the opening number. And then the not so bright foyer I'd been frogmarched out to, and the dimly lit cab I'd taken back home where I drowned my sorrows in a bottle (or two or three, but who's counting?) of chardonnay. It dawns on me, my dream wasn't a dream, but my reality.

I smack my lips together, just now realising how dry my mouth is. Rolling my head to the side, I peek through slit eyes once again to see if I'd remembered to leave a water on my bedside table. It appears I not only had the forethought to place an ice-cold glass of water by my bed, but also two Tylenol and a half-eaten burrito.

"You want the good news, or the bad?" Cybil appears out of nowhere wearing a bright yellow pant suit that could rival Hilary Clinton. I blink against the glare, reaching a shaky hand towards the glass.

"What time is it?" My voice sounds as though I smoked my way through a carton of cigarettes and washed it down with broken glass.

"Noon. Here." She picks up the Tylenol and hands them to me. "You look like shit. Have a little pity party for one, did we?"

I glare at her as I down the pills with a big gulp of water. My eyes land on the burrito and I wonder if it's still any good.

Cybil folds her hands across her ample chest. "I wouldn't. Not unless you feel like a dose of food poisoning on top of your hangover." Her raised eyebrow seems almost like a challenge, but I decide not to tempt fate today. Though really, if my memory serves me correctly, things couldn't possibly get any worse.

I drag my body farther up the bed to lean against the headboard. "Let's have it. Have I ruined everything?" My shaky hands find their way to my temple, pressing ever so gently to try and ease the thumping.

Cybil stalks over to her briefcase and retrieves a handful of newspapers. She throws them on my bed and resumes her headmistress stance; arms folded across her chest, pursed lips, eyes peering at me over her wire-rimmed glasses.

"That bad, huh?" I wince, afraid to look.

She picks one up and waves it about. "*Drunk and disorderly.*" She throws it back on the pile and grabs another. "*Drunk debacle at the Oscars.*" That one lands on top and another is held in the air. "And my personal favorite, *Emma's Jonesing for another drink.*" The paper lands on the heap, and she places her hands on her hips, staring at me with her raised brow.

I can't help but mimic her. "Come on, Cybil. What's the old adage? There's no such thing as bad publicity? Isn't that how it goes?"

"You ran off with Emma Stone's Oscar! I'd say that counts as bad publicity, wouldn't you?"

"At least they'll remember my name?" I shrug, wanting to put an end to this very loud conversation. It's too early, and I'm too hungover to deal with this shit. Isn't that what a publicist is for? To fix my fuck ups?

Cybil huffs and gathers up the papers. "Do you ever take anything seriously?"

"It was an honest mistake. I heard them say Emma Jones." I say my name slowly, exaggerating every syllable.

She straightens up, looking me square in the eye. "You really heard that?"

I nod. "I really heard that." I take another sip of water, blanching at the blandness. "The rest just kinda happened. I panicked." I shrug again, letting out a long sigh. "I fucked up."

"Damn right you did. It's going to take some serious ass-kissing to fix this, you know that, right?"

"I know." I lower my head, not because I'm remorseful, but because the image of Cybil kissing anyone's ass is enough to make me laugh.

"I'm heading in to the office to see if I can make some headway with this." She holds the papers in the air as she marches towards the door. "The journalists are having a field day, so be prepared to have your dirty laundry aired out for everyone to see."

"I don't have any—"

"Save it for the press. You know as well as I do, they're vultures. They will tear you apart if you so much as look at them." She drags her glasses from her face, squinting her eyes closed. "I hope, for your sake, they don't find anything. Because if they do, you're in for a lot worse than this lot." Shoving the papers under her arm, she stalks out the door, her heels clacking on the granite tiles of the foyer.

Well, shit. My morning just got off to a great start. I need a fucking drink.

Chapter three

With a Bloody Mary under my belt, I make my way to the large bay window, peeking through the blinds.

Son of a bitch. I knew I should've had a fence installed.

My driveway is still swarming with paparazzi, obviously out to catch a snap of me in another drunken stupor, or worse. I hate it when Cybil is right.

One of them spots me and scurries over the lawn. I wait until she's made it halfway across before flicking a switch and turning the sprinklers on. The look on her face is priceless as she spins on her heels, deciding which way to run. I snort, watching her scamper back to the safety of the asphalt. When she turns to glare at me, I lift my hand and offer a condescending wave followed by my middle finger. Vulture.

Satisfied she got the message, I let my robe fall open as I meander down the hall toward my bathroom. The stench of last night's bender still clings to my skin and I feel an overwhelming desire to scrub myself raw. Perhaps if I rub hard enough, my little faux pas will disappear, and the press will leave me alone. Pfft. Perhaps pigs will grow wings and learn to fly.

I disrobe in front of the full-length mirror, taking stock. Legs, check. Boobs, check. Face... has seen better days. Apparently so have my arms; a large purple bruise sits just above my elbow.

What in hell did I get up to last night?

A brief image of me halfway up a tree flits through my brain and is gone before I can really focus on it. At this point, I'm just happy I even managed to make it home in one piece.

After twisting this way and that, looking at myself from every angle possible, I slip into the shower. Hot water stings my flesh, raining down my back and making me feel somewhat human again. With a sponge lathered in sweet-smelling body wash, I scrub until my skin is red. Maybe one day I'll scrub hard enough that I won't want to drink again. Today is not that day.

It's going to take a bucket load of grog to get me through this. I think I might be suffering from PTSD or something. Every time I blink, I see those damn camera flashes behind my eyes, followed by the image of the Oscar flying from my hands.

God, what was I thinking? This is Hollywood, and shit sticks in Hollywood. I'll be forever known as the drunk woman who stole an Oscar. Not just any Oscar, but Emma Stone's Best Actress Oscar. My head falls into my hands and I let out a low groan. When I hopped on a plane to the US of A almost three years ago, I never imagined my life would turn out this way. The first few months were hell. I struggled to find work and was on the bones of my ass until, by some miracle, Cybil came into my life, and I landed the role of Macie Sweetwater, the entrepreneur our movie was based on. And then came the offers. I was Hollywood's new sweetheart of the screen. With money flowing in, and drinks on a never-ending carousel, it wasn't long before I began needing a drink to start the day. And then another to get through the middle of the day. Pretty soon I was on more of a liquid diet than anything else. I suppose I should've seen it coming; the beginning of my demise. I guess it was fun while it lasted. I only wish I could've done a little more before my time was up. Just one more night in the spotlight.

A muffled-sounding imperial march comes from the heap of clothes on the floor, pulling me from my thoughts. That can only mean one thing. Cybil is calling.

I take my time rummaging through them, not really caring if I miss her call. I'm not in the mood for another lecture, and considering she's already been up my ass this morning, I can only assume more shit has hit the fan.

What could it be this time?

Pressing the green button to accept her call, I muster my cheeriest of voices. "Cybil! Long time, no see!"

"Emma, I don't know how you did it, but you've been called in for an audition."

"Seriously?" I sit up, a grin slowly forming on my face. "I should get drunk and disorderly more often."

I can almost hear her eyes rolling as she takes a deep breath. "It's not a significant role, but considering the circumstances, it's more than I expected."

Ignoring her attempt to insult me, I keep up the cheery disposition. "Great! It'll be nice to take a backseat role between jobs. Keep things interesting." With a bounce in my step, I head for my room to pick out some clothes. "When's the audition?"

"That's the thing. It's today."

"Today? Who holds auditions the day after the Oscars?" My head's still not feeling the best after last night's soiree.

Brushing over my question, she continues. "Can you be at Burbank Boulevard at 5pm?"

I stop in my tracks. "Burbank Boulevard? Did you just say Burbank freaking Boulevard? As in *Universal Studios*? I'm auditioning for Universal Studios?" It's like a dream come true! I don't care how small the role is, if Universal wants me to, I'll sweep the damn floors!

"It's not Universal."

I watch my excitement deflate and fly around the room like a burst balloon. "Oh."

"It's across the road and down a bit. They're a relatively new set-up called Rampage Productions."

"Well, I guess I can see why they want me then; the rampaging actress of the Oscars." An unladylike snort bursts forth as I chuckle, and I just know Cybil is cringing. She really won the jackpot when she agreed to sign me up two years ago.

"Hmmm." She has her disappointed headmistress voice on again. "Just make sure you're there, okay? We need to jump on this while we can, and maybe, just maybe, you'll walk out of this unscathed."

The phone clicks as I'm dismissed. Her abrasive nature is what drew me to her in the first place. I guess she reminds me a little of home. She calls a spade a spade, and she doesn't take shit from anyone. A no-nonsense kind of woman who isn't afraid to kick my ass if I need it. Admittedly, I thought that after two years she might've warmed up to me a little more, but we can't have it all, and she hasn't steered me wrong yet. In fact, she's probably the only person in this crazy town that I trust wholeheartedly.

Which is why I won't let her down today. Not even the press will stop me from making this audition.

Chapter four

With my oversized sunglasses on, and a scarf covering my head, *Thelma and Louise* style, I duck into the garage. Thank God I'd had the forethought to buy a place with internal access.

My pink Rolls Royce, Betsy, is sitting smack bang in the middle, leaving plenty of room either side – can't be putting a ding in that pretty little thing. Aside from my house, it was my one big purchase when I got my first substantial pay check. As a girl, I'd dreamed of owning a car like Lady Penelope, and as expensive as it was, it is worth every damn penny. This baby is my pride and joy.

Of course, there's no sneaking around in a car like this. One look at the sleek, pink body and the chrome grill, and they'd know it was me; especially after *Entertainment Weekly* did a piece about the new Lady Penelope in town.

Which is why I'd asked Dawn to meet me out on the street. It's a risky move, but with the paparazzi on my doorstep, I don't have a lot of options.

Dawn is my publicist. Her and Cybil don't always see eye to eye, but they both have my best interests at heart. Unlike Cybil, Dawn is more of a free spirit. She can often be found in yoga pants and flowing tops, with beads in her dreadlocked hair, and a multitude of bangles adorning her arms. She may not be the best at her job, but she's fun to have around. What she lacks in professionalism, she more than makes up for in attitude. Which is exactly why she is the one I called to help me out of this jam. Sure, she should be making sure my reputation stays golden right now, but I think Cybil has it covered. One of them has to.

When I realized I'd have to try and sneak past the press, Dawn was the first person I thought of. She's always up for a bit of an adventure, and what could be more exciting than evading the press?

Together, we came up with a plan. Not a very good one, but a plan all the same. I am to duck through the back door in the garage, skirt around the side of the lap pool, and slip through the hedge on the other side. From there, I should be able to walk down the small alley between me and the neighbour, before breaking out onto the street. Dawn will be waiting there in her beat-up '79' BMW, ready to drive like a bat out of hell to get me across town to the audition in time. Easy.

That was the plan. However, now that I'm standing in my garage, staring out at the overgrown hedge I'm meant to get through, I'm not so sure this was thought through enough. I've only been in this house a few months, if you don't count when I'm on set, and the gardens have never really held my interest – I plan on hiring a gardener for that sort of thing. Me and dirt don't mix well. Never have, never will. Of course, I probably should've taken all this into account when I devised this plan, because from where I'm standing, it's not looking good. Red berries cover the hedge, and if I'm not mistaken, those berries are protected by small barbs.

I look down at my white silk blouse. This is not going to end well.

With no time to change, I tip toe over to Betsy and ever so quietly open the back door to retrieve a picnic blanket I keep stowed under the backseat – you never know when an impromptu picnic may arise. Wrapping it around my shoulders to protect my blouse, I push the door closed with a gentle click and pad over to the far corner of the room. Peering out the window, I see no signs of the paparazzi on this side of the house, so I slip through the door, pulling it quietly closed behind me.

Removing my heels, I do a stealth run – and by stealth run, I mean more of a gallop – around the pool to the hedge. I pull the blanket tight around my shoulders, and fling my back against the shrubbery, making sure no one has spotted me yet. So far, so good.

I drop to my knees, searching for a way into the bush, but it appears to be denser than I thought, and those barbs are a lot longer and pointier than I was expecting. I don't like my chance of getting through. Especially when I can't even make out the light of day on the other side. This brings me to yet another conclusion; that hedge backs onto a concrete wall.

Damn it.

With a curse under my breath, I peer over my shoulder to check that I'm still in the clear before turning my gaze up to the top of the bush. It doesn't look *that* high.

I take a quick swig of my 'emergency brew' I keep in my purse. Nothing like a bit of Dutch courage to help me out of a bind.

The blanket quickly becomes a knapsack for my heels, and I sling it around my neck and under one arm to hold it in place. I send a silent prayer to the big man upstairs, begging for a little help as I attempt to climb this overgrown thorn bush.

My skinny jeans provide some protection from the barbs, but my hands and feet are screaming out at me to move faster. I'm too afraid to look at my blouse after hearing the distinct sound of fabric ripping.

Must push on.

Somehow, I reach the top and manage to swing my legs over the edge. What I didn't count on, however, is that a concrete wall is just that; a concrete bloody wall! Unlike a climbing wall in a gym, this one does not have handy little foot holds, just a sheer face that seems a hell of a lot higher now that I'm up here.

I spy a patch of greenery to my right, and throw my shoes and blanket over that way, in hopes that it will soften the fall. Shimmying my butt along the wall to line myself up with the lush foliage, I keep reminding myself why I'm doing this.

I fucked up, and this job will help to give me credibility again.

Cybil is counting on me to be there. My ass is well and truly on the line here.

Just a few more inches...

"Emma! Em—"

Fuck a duck.

My foot slips out from under me as the press runs towards me, screaming my name. I lose my balance, and my back scrapes along the edge of the wall as I manoeuvre myself mid-air to grab hold of the lip with my fingertips. With my face pressed into the cool concrete block, and my feet dangling somewhere above and to the left of that nice soft piece of shrubbery, I let out a squeak, which turns into a chuckle. Only I could royally screw this up to this proportion.

Craning my neck side to side, I attempt to shuffle sideways to at least be able to throw myself at the grass and not the asphalt, but once again, I lose my grip and slide in a very unladylike fashion, down the wall. Closing my eyes, I prepare myself for the bone-crushing landing. But it never comes. Instead, I find a strong set of arms wrapped around my waist, and a warm chest at my back.

"I've got you," a husky voice mutters in my ear.

"You bet you do," I murmur as I slide down his body to the ground. His hands rest on my hips, steadying me while I take stock.

My jeans are dusty, my blouse is torn down the bottom with smears of red berry juice across my middle, and my hands have seen better days. Still, not as bad as it could have been without my savior coming to the rescue.

Smoothing my hands down my front, I lift my head and spin around to face my knight in shining armor.

His firm chest is at eye level, and as I sweep my eyes up, I can't help but notice the square set to his jaw, and the light dusting of stubble. His piercing blue eyes stare down at me with a hint of amusement.

"Thank you," I say in a voice much like Marilyn Monroe when she sang *Happy Birthday* to JFK. I can't seem to pull my gaze from his, even though I know I should. I'm supposed to be incognito, and for all I know, this guy could be one of *them*.

"Well, I could hardly leave a lady dangling from my wall now, could I?" he drawls, his southern twang still present.

"This is your... um... yard?" The words come out in a squeak.

Christ, what have I gotten myself into? And what the hell is wrong with my voice?

His chuckle rumbles through his chest. "In a sense." He reaches down to retrieve my shoes and blanket. "I believe these are yours."

Clearing my throat, I take hold of the items. "Uh, yeah. Thanks. Again." I wave them in the air with a little laugh. "I should probably be going..." I turn away from him but pull up short when my eyes land on the sweeping mansion before me.

Apparently, I don't pay much attention to my surroundings at all.

"Road's that way, ma'am." He points in the opposite direction, a smirk across his handsome face.

"Right. Of course." I nod as if I'd known it all along. "I'll be off then, Mr..." I trail off, realizing I don't know his name.

"Brock Appleby, at your service." He holds a large, weathered hand out to me.

A man with hands like that certainly knows how to use them.

Just the thought of what those hands could do has tingles running through my body. I reach out, slipping my dwarf-like hand in his. The rough callouses on his palm rub against my soft skin, and again, my mind wanders onto images of his hands trailing my body.

"And you are?" he prompts, his voice jolting me from my trance. I lift my gaze to meet his.

He has no idea who I am.

After last night, I didn't think that was possible.

"Emma." I smile up at him, holding his hand a little longer than necessary.

A horn blasts down the long drive, and I know Dawn is waiting. I'd recognize that sound anywhere. She installed one of those tacky horns that plays a ditty every time she pushes the button. She can even select a different tune depending on her mood. Right now, it's *La Cucaracha*.

"That's my ride." I hook my thumb over my shoulder, slowly backing away from him. "It was lovely meeting you, Brock." His name falls from my tongue as if it was always meant to be there.

"Likewise, Miss Emma." Something about the way he speaks has me picturing him riding bareback and tipping his hat at me like one of those old-timey western cowboys. He's like a wholesome, boy-next-door only with less emphasis on the boy, and more on the man. The hot, manly man. My new house just got a whole lot more interesting.

Chapter five

"You realize that horn is less than subtle, right?" I say as I climb into the front seat. "We're supposed to be sneaking away, not drawing attention to ourselves."

Dawn waves a hand in the air. "To-may-toe, To-mah-toe." She shifts the gearstick and swerves out onto the road, narrowly avoiding a cyclist.

"*Not* drawing attention, Dawn." I shake my head. For a publicist, she really has no clue how to handle herself in public. Possibly the reason why I'm her only client, and by client, I mean I pay her and she occasionally works. That's pretty much our dynamic. She's like that friend who never has any money, so you end up paying all the time, only, it comes in the form of a weekly wage.

"My driving is the least of your worries, sugar." She purses her lips as she looks me up and down. "Don't think I didn't see your little stunt last night."

"Oh, you saw that, huh?"

"Mmhmm. Honey, I think everyone saw what you did." Dragging her eyes back to the road, she lets out a chuckle. "It certainly livened up the show, that's for damn sure!"

"That's one way of looking at it."

"Oh, hush." She reaches out and pats my hand. "I know Cybil'll be riding you already, I'm not about to give you a lecture too. You know what you did." She looks me in the eye. "Right?"

I nod, huffing out a breath. "Yeah."

"So, what you gonna do about it?"

"Uh... isn't that where you come in?" I quirk a brow. It's certainly what I'm paying you for.

"Uh-uh. You can't go stealing another woman's Oscar and then expect me to clean up your mess."

I kinda thought that was in the job description...

"And that's *not* what I mean anyways." She gives my hand a squeeze. "You know what I'm talking about."

The booze. It's always the booze.

"Yeah, I know. I've got it under control."

"Do you, though?" She fishes around in her bra, pulling out a crumpled business card. "Here. In case you decide you're ready."

"What's this, Dawn? An intervention? Jesus. I expected this from Cybil, but not from you." I snatch the card from her hand. "So I got a little drunk. It was one night. It won't happen again."

"Mmhmm. And this isn't a weave." She flicks her hand through her coloured dreadlocks.

I gasp and throw a hand across my chest? "It's not?"

Her lips pull up into a smirk. "Quit playing, girl. You know I'm only trying to look out for you." Her eyes flick to mine briefly. "I worry about you."

And just like that, I feel like shit. For all her flaws, Dawn has been like a mother to me. A slightly misguided mother, but a mother all the same. "I know." I wrap my arms around her as best I can and kiss her cheek. "Thank you for looking out for me."

"It's my pleasure, honey." She reaches up and pats my arm still draped around her. "Now, where are we headed? You auditioning for a murder victim role?"

"I don't think so. Why?"

She glances out the corner of her eye. "Uh, because you look like you've been attacked by a chainsaw." She waves her hand up and down, gesturing to my torn clothing.

I reach my hand up and try to smooth my hair back. "That bad, huh?"

"Honey, your shirt's all torn to shreds, your hair has got an afro vibe going on, and you're not wearing any shoes." She raises a brow. "You telling me you didn't look like that when you left home? Should I be worried?"

"Believe it or not, I actually looked respectable when I left. It's not an easy job to evade the press when they're on your doorstep, Dawn. I had to scale a barbed hedge and take a flying leap from the top."

A little embellishment never hurt anyone.

"You jumped from up there? Girl, you're crazy! You could've broken your damn neck!"

"Believe me, it wasn't exactly part of the plan. And anyway, a big, burly man came to my rescue." I can't help the grin that spreads across my face at the thought of Brock's strong hands on my waist.

"Big and burly, eh?" She chuckles. "You always land on your feet, don't you?"

"I like to think so." We approach an intersection and I point Dawn in the right direction.

"You gonna tell me where we're goin? Or do I have to guess?"

"Burbank Boulevard. Some place called Rampage Productions?" I shrug. "It's only a bit part, but I'll take anything right now."

"Rampage Productions. That's the Ramirez brothers, isn't it?"

I shake my head and purse my lips. "I have no idea. I've never heard of it before. Cybil said they're a new studio." Pulling my phone out, I do a quick search. "Rampage Productions, an up and coming studio run by brothers, Blake and Bo Ramirez. After winning a Cannes Film Festival award for Best Short Film for their debut movie, *All About Frank* in May of 2017, all eyes are on them to see what they will produce next." Looking up from my phone, I nod. "Sounds like they know what they're doing."

"Mmm, just be careful with them, sugar. Make sure you have Cybil check everything over before you go signing your life away."

"I always do."

She shoots me a sharp look. "I mean it. You know who their father is, right? You don't want to get messed up in anything he's a part of."

"Why? Who's their father? This sounds juicy." I spin my body around to face her, tucking my foot under my knee.

"Marty Ramirez, the right-hand man of Al Breakwell." When I continue to stare at her in confusion, she sighs. "Honey, where the hell have you been? You never heard of the Breakwell murders?"

"Murders?"

"Mmmhmm. Everybody knows it was him and his hired hands, but they can't pin anything on him, because Marty is the one turning the crank in the background. He's the smarts, and Al is the face."

"So, let me get this straight. I'm about to audition for the brothers of a man *behind a man* wanted for murder?" I huff out a breath. "Shit, that's... Shit."

"I don't mean to scare you, I just want you to be careful is all. Word is, they're trying to go on the straight and narrow, but you never know who's pulling the strings behind the scenes."

"Right, well, thanks for scaring the bejeebus out of me. Don't suppose you've got any clean knickers in the back there?" I peer over my shoulder at the back seat laden with clothes.

"Joke all you want, missy, just heed my warning. Don't get into bed with the Ramirez brothers unless you know for damn sure you've got an out." Her deep brown eyes meet mine. "That's all I'll say on the matter."

We pull onto Burbank Boulevard, and I can't help but fix my eyes on Universal Studios as we drive slowly by.

One day.

A few blocks down, I spot the small building with Rampage Productions scrawled out front.

After what Dawn just told me, I'd half expected it to be a run-down building in a dodgy neighbourhood, not this tidy, well-kept establishment before me. Silly, I know. Burbank Boulevard is hardly a dodgy neighbourhood. It's the home of one of the greatest film production companies of all time.

"Well, this is it." I unbuckle my seatbelt and turn to face her. "Wish me luck."

"Knock 'em dead, sugar." She smiles but it doesn't quite meet her eyes. "I'll be right here if you need me." She reaches over and grabs her kindle from the glove compartment. "Nicole Goodin just released her new book *Hide and Seek* and I've been dying to know what happens with Jasper Jones and Hannah Montgomery."

I laugh and shake my head as I step out of the car. "You and your love stories."

"Don't knock 'em till you try 'em." She swipes her finger across the screen and settles back in her chair. "Go on now." She waves a hand towards me. "Go get yourself a piece of the action."

Chapter six

"Emma Jones to see the casting directors please. I believe they're expecting me." I plaster a smile on my face and smooth my hand through my hair once more as the young receptionist peers up at me from behind her computer screen. If she knows who I am, she hides it well.

"Yes, of course, Miss Jones. If you'll take a seat, I'll let them know you've arrived." She points a manicured finger towards the waiting area, and I nod, making my way over to the seats but not sitting. Instead, I wander around the room, looking at the framed pictures on the wall. The Ramirez brothers certainly get around. Their mugs are plastered all over these walls with every celebrity imaginable. On the red carpet of the Oscars, with the stars on Hollywood Boulevard, and if I'm not mistaken, in the sound room at Jamie Foxx's place. I've never been there myself, but I've certainly heard all about it. Anyone who's anyone goes there at some point in their career. I think *my* invite got lost in the mail.

"Miss Jones." A tall drink of water steps out from a door down the hall. He eyes my torn blouse with amusement but says nothing. "Thank you for coming on such short notice." He strides forward, his arm extended. "I'm Blake Ramirez, and this is my brother, Bo." He indicates to the man following behind. Up close and personal, their looks are almost identical. The only thing separating them, the color of their eyes. Blake has hazel eyes with flecks of green, whereas Bo has deep, chocolate brown.

I accept his offered hand. Unlike Brock's, his skin is smooth and soft; the hands of an executive type. "Nice to meet you. I've heard good things."

Bo barks out a laugh. "I'm sure you have. Our reputation is nothing if not 'good'." He slaps Blake on the shoulder. "You're good here?"

Without taking his eyes off me, Blake nods. "Of course. I'm sure Miss Jones and I can handle this."

"Right then." Bo steps forward. "I'll leave you in the capable hands of my brother. It was a pleasure to meet you." His eyes sparkle as he throws me a wink and walks out the door.

"If you'll follow me, Miss Jones."

"Please, call me Emma."

"Emma." Placing his hand on the small of my back, he ushers me down the hall and through another door. "You can pop your bag down over there. Have you had a chance to look over the script?"

"Yes, briefly."

"Good." He nods. "I'd like to have you read the part of Taylor, and we'll go from scene four." He grabs a script and moves out onto the floor. "I'll read Matt's lines."

"Oh, okay." I thumb through the pages to find the right scene, then walk out to join him. "Wait, Taylor is the lead. I thought I was reading for Rebecca?"

"Change of plans. My leading lady fell through, and I think you'd be perfect for her."

Holy shit. Another leading role. I do my best not to jump up and down in excitement.

Schooling my features, I change the subject. "So, do you always read the parts with your auditionees?"

"Most of the time, yes. I get a better feel for it this way." He turns to the front, shielding his eyes from the spotlight. "You ready over there, Javier?"

"Ready when you are."

"Emma?"

"Ready."

He holds a finger in the air and whirls it around to signal the start of filming.

I close my eyes and take a deep breath, getting into character. One wobbly foot in front of the other, I walk towards Blake. "Hey, baby."

"You're drunk."

"Pssh." I wave a hand in the air. "Nooooo." I stumble and fall into his arms with a giggle. "Okay, maybe juss a lil bit."

"Jesus, Taylor, how'd you get home? Please tell me you didn't drive."

"Ummm." Sucking my lips in, I pull my finger and thumb across my mouth like a zip. "Wooden you like ta know."

He takes hold of my arms, shaking me. "You realize you could've killed someone, or worse, yourself! What about the kids?"

"Don't be like that. I'm fiiiiiine."

"No, you're not." He turns his back, his head cradled in his hands. "I can't do this anymore."

"Whaddaya mean? Matt?" With a shake of his head, he walks away. "Matt! You can't just leave!"

"Aaaand cut."

My heart pounds as it always does when I'm performing, and I have to close my eyes to center myself again.

Blake steps back into the light. "Emma, that was great. Thank you. I'll discuss it with Bo and we'll be in touch."

"You don't want me to do it again?" I'm so used to doing scenes over with a different emphasis, that it throws me a little.

"No, I think I've seen all I need to see. That was perfect." He smiles, and it's enough to wash away my insecurity.

"Right. Okay."

"Hang on a sec, I'll walk you out."

I gather my belongings and wait by the door while he talks to the camera guy. Propping myself up against the door frame, I watch their interaction.

They seem comfortable together. I would even go so far as to say, they're equals, rather than employee and employer. It's nice to see that he treats his staff with the same amount of respect. It's a quality to admire. Especially in this business.

I've met my fair share of snooty producers who look down on their team, as if they're barely good enough to wipe their boots on. But not Blake. He seems to genuinely be interested.

And he wants you as his leading lady.

I'm not sure if I should be flattered or bothered that he thinks I'd be perfect for the role of a drunk, but as Cybil pointed out, I can't afford to be picky right now.

Don't get into bed with the Ramirez brothers unless you know for damn sure you've got an out.

Dawn's words ring in my ears as Blake saunters towards me, but I can't get my brain to connect the man before me with what she'd warned about.

There's something about Blake Ramirez that has me drawn to him. I don't care what the rumor mill says, Blake is nothing like his father, of that I'm sure.

Chapter seven

By the time I make it home, all but one reporter is gone from my doorstep. Instantly, I recognize her from this morning. Her wash in the sprinkler obviously wasn't enough to send her packing. She's got determination, I'll give her that. Still, I duck my head and push forward. The call of alcohol is strong, and my 'emergency stash' was finished before I'd even made it back to Dawn's car.

"Miss Jones, what are your thoughts on how you were man-handled by the Academy last night?"

Without breaking my stride, I answer with a, "no comment."

"Really? You have no comment on being marched out of the building? It's hardly the way to treat an A-lister." She's hot on my heels, and when I spin to face her, she almost runs into me, but stumbles backwards, catching herself.

Wait, did she just say A-lister?

"Are you going to be pressing charges?"

I frown, scrunching my nose. "Why would I press charges?"

Mayday, mayday! Fraternizing with the enemy!

"Why *wouldn't* you press charges? They put their hands on you, in front of witnesses I might add, and marched you out of there like a criminal. Haven't you seen the papers?"

Don't answer her. Do. Not. Do. It.

"I... hadn't really thought of it that way."

Abort! Abort! Cybil's number one rule – Don't admit anything to the press!

"You really should start thinking of it that way. They painted you as some kind of villain, when it was really just a misunderstanding." She steps in, pushing her wire-framed spectacles further up on her nose. "I could help you fix your reputation."

And there it is.

I fold my arms across my chest. "That so? And how do you plan on doing that?"

"By doing an exclusive on you. Let them see the you you want them to see, not the you that was plastered all over the news and papers." Her fingers flick the page of her notebook over, a pencil poised at the ready. She's old school, but I like it.

"And how do I know you won't do the same thing as all the others? Hmm? Why should I trust you?"

"Well, because I know what it's like to have your name dragged through the mud. Maybe not on a scale as big as this, but I bet it still hurts just the same." Her voice is softer, more vulnerable. She's either sincere, or she's in the wrong business.

Clearing her throat, she rummages through her bag, pulling out a card. "Here. You can look me up if you like, see that I'm not after the glory. I just want to tell *your* story."

I hesitate, knowing Cybil will kick my ass for even thinking this over. My curiosity gets the better of me though, and I take the proffered card. Her hand wraps around mine briefly.

"I'm on your side, Miss Jones. Just think it over." Without so much as a second glance, she turns on her heels and struts back down the drive.

I stare at the name on the card. Sydney Marshall. The name doesn't ring any bells, but I rarely pay attention to the tabloids, let alone who's writing them.

She has me intrigued though. Something about the way she spoke gave me chills, and I can't help but feel that she's the real deal, and in this business, that's not easy to come by.

***

After my long, arduous day of avoiding the press, listening to lectures on my behavior, and my five-minute audition with Blake, I feel the need for a large cocktail and a soak in the bath. Rummaging through the cupboards, I find a bottle of Smirnoff, surprisingly almost full, a tiny dribble of peach schnapps and enough orange juice to scrape together a close cousin to a Sex on the Beach.

I pull the curtains closed in the sitting room, and head through to the bathroom with both the vodka and my cocktail. Clearing off the little side table I keep in here for such instances, I carefully place my beverages down while I draw the bath and light some candles. A flicker of movement out the window catches my attention, and I quickly drop the lighter down on the vanity and make my way down the hall to the garage. Standing on tippy toes, I peer out the window that looks over the garden. A knock on the side door nearly gives me a heart attack, and I jump backwards ten feet, holding my hand to my chest.

"Sorry, Miss Emma. I didn't mean to startle you." Brock stands at the door with that boyish grin on his face. He lifts the brim of his hat and dabs at his forehead with a handkerchief before placing it back down again.

A girly giggle slips out of my lips as I saunter over to the door as if I hadn't just had the scare of my life. With a gentle push, I swing the door open. "Hi, Brock. What are you doing here?"

"I hope you don't mind, but I thought your bush could do with a trim."

"I'm sorry, what?" I blink, opening my eyes wide as I wait for him to elaborate.

A soft blush colors his cheeks as he peers down at me. "The... uh... bush." He points over his shoulder, then continues. "I noticed your blouse was torn up this morning after you scaled the fence, and I thought you might like it trimmed."

He lifts the brim of his hat again, swiping the back of his hand across his forehead. "I didn't mean to intrude, or to cause offense, ma'am."

I wave my hand dismissively. "The only offense I'm taking is the use of the word *ma'am*. I'm not that old." I throw him a wink then admonish myself for being so cheesy. *Who winks these days?*

He chuckles, and I get a glimpse of a tiny dimple in his cheek. *Could this guy be any dreamier?*

"Excuse me, ma... Uh, Miss Emma. My granddaddy always taught me to treat women with respect."

"Your granddaddy sounds like a great man. And thank you... For the bush. That's very sweet of you."

"It's my pleasure." He holds his hand across his heart and tips his head, his eyes never leaving mine. I lean a shoulder on the door frame, twirling a loose strand of hair around my finger. We stand this way for a few seconds before he turns his head towards the drive. "I best be on my way. I'll leave you to your evening."

"No, wait." I reach out and touch his arm before I can stop myself. His muscles flex under my fingers. My eyes automatically drift to where our skin touches, and a myriad of thoughts race through my mind about how good we'd look together; his bronze skin against my alabaster. We'd make a striking couple on the red carpet.

He clears his throat. "Miss Emma?"

My eyes dart back up to his, and I withdraw my hand. "Sorry, I was a million miles away." My cheeks heat up, and I'm sure they're a lovely shade of crimson; the one drawback to having skin so pale.

He chuckles, making his eyes crinkle at the sides in a sexy George Clooney kind of way.

Stop being such a perv and say something!

"Let me get you some money for your trouble," I manage to say.

"No need for that, Miss Emma. Think of it as a favor."

"No, no, no." I shake my head. "I insist." I step through the door, ushering him inside.

"Really, it's no bother."

I cock my hip and fold my arms across my chest. "And it's no bother for me to pay you."

"You're not going to take no for an answer, are you?" He grins, and I very nearly melt into a puddle on the floor.

Straightening my blouse, I say, "Nope," then wink before turning my back to him, cringing. *Again with the winking! What the hell, Emma?*

I take two steps before I realize something isn't right. The carpet squelches beneath my feet, and upon inspection, I see a giant wet patch snaking down the hall.

The bath!

"Oh shit!" I take off for the bathroom in a sort of gallop. Water cascades over the side of the bath, soaking the floors. Without thinking, I run in to turn off the faucet, only my bare feet slip on the wet linoleum floor and suddenly my legs are flying out in front of me. Before I land in a heap on the sopping floor, two strong arms once again come to my rescue, catching me.

"We're gonna have to stop meeting like this," I say as he helps me to my feet. "I'm really not normally this clumsy."

Once I'm upright and steady, he strides into the bathroom and turns the water off, while I stand there admiring his ass as he bends over.

Nice.

"Do you have some towels we can use to clean this up?" He turns to me with a questioning look.

"Uh, yeah. In the cupboard over there." I point across the room. "But I can do it. You've done so much already." I slosh over to where he's standing, placing my hand on his arm again.

Any excuse.

"Just let me lay some on the floor real quick, and then I can grab you that money."

"Miss Emma—"

"Please, just Emma."

He nods with a small smile. "Okay, Emma. Please let me help you." He nods at the cocktail and bottle of vodka awaiting my return. "Forgive me for saying, it looks like you've had a rough day." He shrugs.

A shrill laugh bursts from my lips as I quickly gather the glass and bottle in my arms. For the first time, I'm embarrassed to be caught with this much booze. "I was just... um... Sampling this new brand of—" I turn the bottle to face me, realizing my error but continuing anyway, "—Smirnoff vodka for..." *Think damn it!* "An endorsement!"

He raises a brow at me. "Smirnoff vodka? Can't say I've heard of it before." He grins, and somehow that makes me feel better even though I know it's a lie.

"I'll just put these over here." I place them on the vanity. "Are you sure you don't mind helping?"

"It would be my pleasure."

Chapter eight

"You sure I can't interest you in another drink?" I wave the bottle in the air as I lean against the doorframe. After he'd helped me clean up the bathroom, I'd made him stay for a tipple as a thank you. He still refused to take any money from me, no matter what I said.

"Perhaps another time. I've got to be up early in the morning."

"Okay, well, thanks again for trimming my bush and helping me with my waterworks." I snort, then cover my nose with my hand as I giggle. "Pretend you didn't hear that."

"Hear what?" He grins, stepping down onto the drive. "Have a good night, Emma."

"You too, Brock." I watch him walk away while taking a swig straight from the bottle. The smooth liquid barely touches the sides, sending a warmth radiating through my body. While it was nice to have some company for a change, the liquor had been singing its siren song, calling out to me. With no one to witness it, and let's face it, judge me, I can relax with my one true weakness.

With a sigh, I kick the door closed and saunter through to my bedroom. I have everything I need in here. My bottle of Smirnoff, a plush duvet with a collection of soft cushions, and my favorite series, Banshee, on Netflix. I'm a little bit obsessed with Antony Starr. Not only is he hot, but the fact he is a fellow kiwi actor helps to relieve my homesickness some too.

I kick off my heels and climb onto my bed, still unmade from this morning. I'm not interested in having someone come in and do my housework for me. No thank you. As far as I'm concerned, it's just another set of eyes watching my every move. Another person I have to try and convince I don't have a problem. And I don't. Not really.

Alcohol is my one and only vise. It's not like I'm out there getting high on acid or whatever the kids are doing these days. It's just a quiet drink or two, in the comfort of my own home. Or at the Oscars...

Nope. I like my privacy too much to hire a housekeeper. I don't feel comfortable having a stranger come into my house, rummaging through my belongings. And knowing my luck, that's exactly what would happen. I'd hire the only maid to be secretly working for the press.

I wouldn't put it past them to try something sneaky like that. They'll do anything to get a story; hide in dumpsters, bombard you in a bathroom, snap pictures from the bushes. It takes a special kind of person to be in the press; no moral code.

My mind wanders back to Sydney. Something flashed in her eyes back there, something real. I get the feeling this is more than just a job for her. It's some kind of a crusade. It makes me wonder what happened to her.

Dragging my laptop over, I do a quick search of her name. Nothing out of the ordinary; Facebook profile, LinkedIn profile, journalism accolades, professional headshots. It's not until I click on the next page that I see it. An article from seven years ago with an image of a girl's face, much like I imagine Sydney would have looked when she was younger. The name is different, but the resemblance is uncanny.

My finger hovers over the mouse as I take another swig of vodka. "What the hell." I shrug, clicking the link.

On the front page of the Salem Guardian, was an article about a young girl named Cindy Marshall who had spoken out about her uncle's abuse. It went on to say that there had been no evidence of such abuse, and as the accused was a well-respected man of the community, and the girl had run away, the courts were deeming it to be fabricated. Her uncle, the newly elected Mayor of Salem, was therefore acquitted.

This is the world we live in. Money and power is all it takes to sweep things under the rug. Which, in a way, is what I'm attempting to do too, I suppose.

Huh. I hadn't thought of it that way before. Perhaps I'm just as bad as this sick bastard who abused his niece; attempting to make the world forget by jumping straight into the next project.

I shake my head. No. There's no hiding what I did. I'm not denying it happened. Only moving forward and putting it behind me. It's a pity the same couldn't be said for poor Cindy.

Unless... Could it be that Cindy and Sydney are one and the same?

I swipe her card up from the dresser, staring at the words as if they'll offer up the truth.

My laptop pings, drawing my attention away. The image of my parents' faces pops up on the screen. This can only mean one thing. They've seen a rerun of last night.

I'm going to need more booze for this.

I quickly down another hefty mouthful before accepting their call.

"Hi, Mom, Dad. How are you?" I plaster a smile across my face and wait for the barrage of questions I know are coming. Mom looks as though she's sucked on a lemon, while Dad tries to hide his smirk.

"Hey, pumpkin." He waves, offering a small smile. "You look well."

Mom tsks and folds her arms across her chest. "What have you got to say for yourself, young lady?"

"Mom, please. I'm an adult."

"Don't you take that tone with me, missy. Your face is all over the papers here, and not in a good way. We can't walk down the street without someone laughing behind our backs." She shakes her head.

"It's not that bad, Jean." Dad shrugs. "I just ignore it."

"Easy for you to say. You can't hear half of what they're saying." She taps her ear and rolls her eyes. Dad's hearing has been slowly deteriorating over the years, but he refuses to do anything about it, saying that hearing aids are for little old men.

I jump in before it becomes an argument. "I'm sorry it's been hard on you, Mom. It was an honest mistake. Our names sound very similar. I thought they said mine."

"And what about the rest? Hmm?" She leans in close to the camera so I get a close up of her nose. "You stole that poor woman's trophy!" she hisses.

I rub my temple with my finger and thumb. "Yeah... I..." I sigh. "I've got no excuse for that."

"The papers say you were drunk. Is that true?" She sits back, her piercing blue eyes boring into mine, disappointment written all over her face. "Do you have a... drinking problem?" Her voice catches in her throat on those last two words.

"No, Mom." My eyes dart to the almost empty bottle of vodka on my dresser as I shake my head. "I promise, I'm fine."

She purses her lips, and if I'm not mistaken, her eyes get a little misty as she turns her head away from me. "We worry about you over there, what with all the drugs and alcohol."

"There's drugs and alcohol everywhere, not just here." She, of all people, knows that.

"You know what I mean. It's more available to you now that you're a big star. I don't want to wake up one day and see you've pulled a Charlie Sheen."

I know she's hurting, so I do what I always do. I play it off as a joke. "I'm not going to upload any crazy videos or lock a hooker in a bathroom, of that you can be sure."

"I think what your mom is trying to say is that we miss you, and we love you, and we hope you're being careful over there," Dad pipes up, wrapping an arm around Mom's shoulder and pulling her close. "We're proud of you, pumpkin."

Mom scoffs, and Dad turns to look at her. "What? She knows I don't mean about last night."

"I know what you mean, Dad. And thank you. It was nice to see your faces." I mean it, too. Sometimes I forget how much I miss them. "I love you."

"We love you too." Mom manages a smile and even blows me a kiss before they end the call.

I close my laptop and push it to the far side of the bed. It's still early enough, so I snuggle down in my duvet, and scroll to my favorites on Netflix, hitting play on season one of *Banshee*. I grab the last of the vodka and slug it back, letting the empty bottle slide from my hands onto the bed beside me, where it will stay until the morning. I can't count the amount of times I've woken up hugging a cold glass bottle to my chest.

No. I don't have a problem at all.

Chapter nine

"Again?" Cybil's disapproving tone wakes me from my slumber. When I peel my eyes open, she's waving the empty bottle of vodka in the air.

"And a hearty good morning to you, too, Cybil," I mumble, pulling myself up. "What are you doing here? In my bedroom. Again." I rub my eyes and stifle a yawn. "You ever heard of a phone?"

She quirks an eyebrow. "Perhaps I wouldn't have to come all the way down here if you'd answer your damn phone once in a while." She drops the bottle in the waste basket by my dresser, then proceeds to rummage through my bed sheets.

"What are you looking for?" I half-heartedly join in on the search.

"Ah." She holds my phone between her forefinger and thumb, as if she might catch something from it. "Flat. I should've known." She stalks over to the wall and plugs it in. "These work a lot better when they're charged." Her sarcasm is out of character, but I roll with it.

"Oh, so that's what it's for! This whole time I thought it was a pretty wall decoration," I drawl.

She peers over her glasses with a stony look. *Someone got out of bed on the wrong side.*

"I had a call from Rampage Productions this morning."

"Oh? And what did Mr. Ramirez have to say for himself?" I fold my hands in my lap to keep from fidgeting while I wait to hear the verdict.

Am I in, or am I out?

"He seemed rather taken by you."

"Really?" I say with a little too much zeal. I drop my voice down an octave. "I mean, really?"

"I believe his exact words were 'she plays a convincing drunk, right down to the clothes she wore'. I don't know what that means, and I don't want to know." She holds a hand up as if warding me off speaking. "But whatever it is you did, he liked it. The part is yours."

My jaw falls open. "I got the part?"

She nods, crossing her hands in front of her. "You got the part." A hint of a smile breaks through her tough demeanor, and it makes this moment even sweeter because I can feel how proud she is.

"I got the part!" I leap to my feet, bouncing on the mattress and sending cushions falling to the floor. It doesn't matter how many parts I get, it's always such a thrill to have my work validated by others. "I got the freakin' part!"

Cybil waves her hands in the air to get my attention. "Yes, you got the part. Now, you just have to keep it." She stalks across the room, retrieving the bottle from the trash. "Which means no more late-night drinking binges." She holds the bottle out to drive her point home.

Snapping my legs together, I pull up straight and salute. "Sir, yes, Sir!"

"I mean it." She pushes her glasses further up on her face, then drops the bottle back in the trash. "We can't have another incident."

With a sigh, I drop down to my knees. "Geez, way to be a downer, Cybil. Can't you at least pretend to be happy for me?"

Her grimace softens, and she steps closer, patting my hand awkwardly. "I *am* happy for you. But it's my job to keep you out of trouble."

"I thought that was Dawn's job."

"Please," she scoffs. "Dawn wouldn't know how to do her job if it jumped up and bit her on the ass. I don't know why you insist on paying her to do nothing."

"It's not nothing. She drove me to the audition yesterday, and she's like my moral support. My cheerleader, if you will." I drop my eyes, finding a loose thread on my duvet. "And, you two were the only ones to give me a chance when I first got here. I couldn't send her packing. We're a team."

"You're throwing your money away on a woman who can barely look after herself, let alone your credibility."

"She's not that bad. In fact, she gave me this yesterday." I slide the crumpled AA business card off my dresser to show her, only Sydney's falls to the floor, landing at Cybil's feet.

"What's this?" She picks it up and immediately turns to me with a raised eyebrow. "You've been talking to the press?"

"No... I mean, not really." I look everywhere but at her.

She folds her arms across her chest and purses her lips. "Not really?" Her tone is clipped.

"She was here when I got home last night, and I couldn't be bothered with the palaver of trying to avoid her." I throw my hands in the air. "So sue me."

"She just might. What did you tell her?"

"Nothing! She did all the talking."

"And?"

"And?" I draw the word out.

"What did she say?"

Letting out a long sigh, I decide to just tell her straight. "She wants to do an exclusive on me and how the Academy handled the situation."

"Of course she does."

"I think she was legit, Cybil. She wasn't like the others out to get whatever they can. She actually seems like she cares." As soon as the words leave my mouth I wince, knowing what's coming my way.

"She's with the press. None of them give a shit about you, Emma. Trust me." She speaks with such disdain, I can't help but wonder if there's a reason for it.

"She had kind eyes." I shrug.

"You make a living out of pretending to be something you're not. You don't think other people can do that too? She's playing you!" She shakes her head, tucking the card in her pocket. "I'm taking this with me. You're too nice for your own good sometimes. You need to harden up if you're really going to make it in this town." She grabs her bag and starts heading for the door.

"I was nominated for an Oscar, I'd say that's me making it in this town, wouldn't you?" I snap back like a petulant child.

She sighs, her head dropping to her chest. "Yes. I suppose you're right."

One Point to me.

"I still stand by what I said. You can't go believing everyone is out to help you. Not everyone is that nice. In fact, most people in this industry aren't. It's dog eat dog out there."

"Well, not everyone is as cynical as you, Cybil. I happen to be a firm believer of treating people as you want to be treated. And I'd rather choose to believe people are generally nice, than out to get me." I climb off the bed and head to my walk-in-robe.

"You keep looking at the world through those rose-tinted glasses and you're going to get one hell of a surprise when you finally take them off and see the world for what it is; a broken place filled with hate and greed."

"Well that's just depressing." I eye her while rifling through my wardrobe for something to wear. "What happened to you to make you see things in such a dismal way? Did you not get hugged enough as a child?" I hold my arms out wide. "You want a cuddle?"

She rolls her eyes. "No, I do not want a cuddle."

"Come on." I purse my lips and wiggle my fingers, beckoning her to me. "Bring it in."

"No." She holds her hand up, shaking her head, while I start moving towards her. "No." Her eyes give her away; a tiny sparkle shining through.

"I know you want to." I step closer. "It'll make you feel better." I pull her into me and her body tenses, her face smooshed into my chest.

"This isn't helping," she says, but her body relaxes into mine, so I squeeze her tighter.

"Shhhh. Just accept it. You're particularly uptight this morning. This'll make the bad feelings go away." I stroke a hand down her hair in a soothing way.

"If I hug you back, will you stop?"

"You know that's what I'm waiting for," I say in a sing-songy voice.

"Ugh, fine." Her arms reach around to pat me on the back. "There. Are we done?"

"Mmmmm." I give one last squeeze before letting her go. "We are now. Feel better?"

She straightens her blazer and fixes her glasses, trying to act like it meant nothing, but I can see her eyes don't look so squinty and tense. "I don't know that better is the right word." She steps back, putting distance between us. "And it still doesn't change things. I stand by what I said. People can be vindictive. Life isn't all about love and light for us all, you know? Some of us have to fight for our right to love who we choose. Some of us have hatred aimed at us wherever we go." She clears her throat and turns towards the door, almost as if she didn't mean to divulge so much, but I'm glad she did. It makes her seem more human, and less like a robot.

"I should go. You need to study your script." She points to the manuscript on my bed, then strides for the door.

"Cybil, wait."

She stops, a hand reaching for the doorframe as if she needs the support. "You don't need to say anything."

"Yes, I do. I'm sorry, okay? I didn't know. You never said..."

"Yeah, well, I try to keep it to myself. You'd be surprised how many closet homophobes there are out there."

"Well, I'm not one of them. Love is love, no matter what flavor."

She bobs her head up and down. "Thanks." When she smiles at me, I see the tears glistening in her eyes. "I wish I could see things the way you do. It would be nice to always see the good in people."

I nod at the trash basket. "Try vodka. It's great at making things seem better than they are." I grin and waggle my eyebrows, but she sighs and rolls her eyes. "No?" I nod. "It's not for everyone."

"And it shouldn't be for you either." She drops her chin and peers at me over her glasses. "You really do need to curb that."

"Okay, Mom. I'll try." I hold up three fingers, plastering a look of pure innocence on my face. "Scouts honor."

Chapter ten

My honor lasted all of an hour. After Cybil left and I'd had a shower, the intoxicating call of the liquor cabinet beckoned. I tried to ignore it, but my brain felt like fuzz and I just needed a little something to sharpen my senses. It's a pity the only thing I have left is an old bottle of vermouth I'd bought to make martinis last Christmas. The flavor isn't so appealing on its own, but I persevere, because I'm not a quitter.

With my glass in one hand, and manuscript in the other, I head to my favorite spot in the house; the bay window in the main sitting room, overlooking the garden. It was the selling point of the house if I'm honest. There's something to be said about curling up in the sun to read a good book, or in this case, script.

Tucking my feet under me, I drag the manuscript onto my lap, ready to dive into my lines. But first, I need another mouthful of my brain juice. Can't learn lines without it.

The dry liquid doesn't do much for my thirst, but it kickstarts my brain with its warming glow. *Ah, booze, you never let me down.*

Flicking the pages open, I skim the set directives and go straight to the part where my character comes in. Right from the word go she's drunk. Not even a lead in, just a hot mess, stumbling through the streets. I flick through to another scene and see that, once again, she's off her face. And in the next. And the next. In fact, it appears she's some form of drunk the entire way through the film.

I set the script down and stare out the window, lifting my glass of vermouth to my lips. Once again, I find myself wondering if I should be offended that this is the role he wants me for. The one he thinks I'm 'perfect for'. Is it because of my actions the other night, or because I'm good at what I do that he thinks this role is made for me?

Needing to mull it over, I pour another glass of the drink that is slowly becoming better with every sip. The more I think about it, the more confused I become. I can virtually see my little alter egos on my shoulders, goading me on.

Angel Emma: *You are an Oscar nominee! He sees your potential.*

Devil Emma: *Or, he sees a helpless drunk who can act.*

Angel Emma: *Exactly. An actor with potential.*

Devil Emma: *Or just a drunk.*

Angel Emma: *An actor who occasionally has a drink or two.*

Devil Emma: *Pfft, one or two dozen, maybe.*

With a shake of my head, I scull back my drink and swipe the script off the seat. "There has to be a scene where I'm not drunk." I keep flicking, page after page, hoping to find even just one tiny scene where I have my act together. It's not until the very end, when I've lost everything, that I finally have a line of sobriety, "Yes, officer."

"Yes, officer? That's it?" I flip the last few pages over, looking for the rest, but come up empty. "You have got to be kidding me!" I throw the script down on the counter and snatch my phone up, my fingers punching the numbers in for Rampage Productions.

"Yes, I'd like to speak to Blake Ramirez, please... No, he's not expecting my call... Yes, I'll hold." I tap my fingers on the counter in time to the elevator music playing in my ear while I wait. Every twenty seconds an automated message informs me that my call is important and to hold for assistance, which is fine the first two times, but after the fifth it's just taking the piss.

"Blake Ramirez." His velvety voice is soothing, and my annoyance subsides somewhat.

Putting on a sultry tone, I try to mimic the message on repeat. "Thank you for waiting. Your call is important to us. Please stay on the line and someone will be with you shortly."

"Ah..."

"Every twenty seconds. Thank you for waiting. Your call is important to us. Please stay on the line and someone will be with you shortly."

"Okay."

"Seriously, Blake. You need to get onto that. It's enough to drive anyone to drink."

"Noted."

"Which brings me to the reason for my call. I think I'm missing some of my script. It just ends on yes, officer. Surely there's more than that." I flick through the pages again to check I'm not imagining it.

"Nope, that's where it ends."

"But... She loses her kids, her job, her fiancé. It can't just end there. Where's the flowers and sunshine? The happy ending?"

His throaty chuckle hums down the line. "There's not always a happy ending, Emma. That's the whole point. Sometimes you do lose everything, and it's only when you reach rock bottom that you realize what you've lost. That's what this is about."

"But, that's..."

"Thought-provoking? Challenging the norm?" he offers.

"I was going to say depressing, but I guess that fits too." I pour the last drop of vermouth into my glass, making a mental note to get more alcohol later. "So, that's really the end? There's no extra scene after the credits? No 'surprise it was just a dream sequence'?"

"I'm sorry to disappoint, but it's really the end. I want to make a difference with our films, not just follow the trends. Stick around long enough and you'll see what I mean." There's a rustling of papers, and he clears his throat. "In fact, there's a gala night for our debut, *All About Frank*, if you'd like to be my plus one. I can introduce you to the man behind the story."

"Oh, uh, I don't know..."

"You've seen the film, right? He's an amazing man. Quite the inspiration."

"I'm sure he is..."

"Come on. It's for a good cause. You'd be doing me a favor."

"Ah..."

"I'll even buy you a drink."

I stare at the empty bottle on my counter, the answer already obvious. "It's a date."

Chapter eleven

In hindsight, another public appearance so soon after the Oscars doesn't seem like such a good idea. If Cybil knew what I was doing, without her having coached me on the do's and don'ts, she'd have a fit. Good thing I decided to keep her in the dark for the time being. I'm not naïve enough to think she won't find out, but by then, the damage will already be done. If I'm lucky, it'll make me look like less of a liability, and more of a respectable member of society. At least, that's what I'm hoping for. That, and a free drink, of course.

The limo pulls up outside the Hollywood Banquet Hall. A red carpet lies between us and the doors, the paparazzi already lined up with their cameras flashing. I swallow back the nerves that have been sitting at the back of my throat the entire journey and plaster on a smile. *Show time.*

"Ready?" Blake slides across the seat, holding his hand out to me.

"Sure." I place my hand in his and again note the softness of his skin. *I must remember to ask what moisturizer he uses.*

The door opens, and we're immediately caught in the camera crossfire. Blake's hand holds firm, guiding me along the carpet as we stop and pose for the press. Before we reach the doors, I hear my name being called, and a reporter pushes his way to the front of the queue to my left.

"Emma, how did it feel to be the laughing stock of the world?"

My lips curl into a grin as I search my brain for a Cybil-acceptable answer. "If I made the world laugh, I must be doing something right, am I right?" Others chuckle beside him, nodding their heads.

He, however, remains unamused by my words. "Mmm, because inebriation is so classy. Tell me, is it true you've got a history of alcohol abuse in your family?"

I stop moving as Blake holds his hand up, coming to my rescue. "Now, that's quite enough. This is a charity event, have some respect." He turns back to me with concern in his eyes. He says something, but I can't tell what as the blood rushes to my ears, blurring all the voices into one.

How.

How did they... I can't even finish my thought before Blake presses a hand to my back and whisks me through the double doors and down a corridor, gently coaxing me into a seat away from prying eyes.

He crouches down before me, his hands resting on my knees. "Emma?" My eyes flick to his. "Are you okay?"

Am I okay? I don't even know how to answer that, so I stare at his thumb as it rubs circles on my lap.

"Do you want to talk about it?"

I shake my head. "No." Pushing the memories back down where I'd buried them, I once again play the part expected of me. "I'm fine, really."

"You sure? You look like you might pass out."

"I haven't really eaten much today, that's probably it." I force a smile on my face and push up from the seat. "I'm fine. Shall we?" I wave a hand towards the dining hall.

Blake watches me for a beat, his eyes full of questions I'm not willing to answer.

"Are you going to escort me, or do I need to find my own way?" I nudge his arm with my shoulder. "I do believe you promised me a drink." I grin as if I'm joking, but all I can think about is getting my hands on a glass of something, anything to dull the ache in my chest, and stop my hands from shaking.

His mouth opens and closes, as if deciding whether to push the issue. With an offer of his elbow, he makes the right decision. "I do believe you're right." He nods his head in a bow. "M'lady."

I nod back with a quirk of my brow. "M'man."

He throws his head back in a throaty laugh, revealing that panty-dropping smile of his. "You're something else, you know that?"

"So I've been told."

He leads me down the corridor to where everyone is converging. Men in black pants and pressed white shirts carry trays of wine. I quickly snatch one from a passing tray, knocking it back, then grabbing another. Blake's eyes are on me, but he doesn't say a word, just gives my arm a squeeze.

I know I should pace myself. I don't want to make another fool out of myself, or worse, Blake, but that reporter caught me off guard and I need a little something to take the edge off.

I can't figure out how he could have got that information when it was meant to be sealed. "Be prepared to have your dirty laundry aired out for everyone to see. I hope, for your sake, they don't find anything. Because if they do, you're in for a lot worse than this lot."

Anything else I could handle, but this? This is hitting below the belt. Even for the press.

"Ah, here he is." Blake's voice cuts into my thoughts. "The man himself." He strides forward, proffering a hand to the sprightly older man coming our way.

"Blake!" The man with silver hair and a cheeky grin waves off Blake's hand, instead pulling him into a hug. "You know better than that." He slaps his hand on Blake's back before pulling back with a glint in his eye. It's almost as though they're sharing a private joke. A joke I wish I was in on. There's something endearing about the little man with a larger-than-life grin.

"Emma, come and meet Frank. Frank, this is Emma, my leading lady."

"Leading lady, eh? So, no hope for this old bloke then?" He winks, grabbing my shoulders and kissing both cheeks.

Blake clears his throat. "Oh, ah, not that kind of leading lady."

"Well, in that case." Frank takes my hand, bringing it to his lips. "Would you do this old man the pleasure of a dance?"

"Oh. Um, no one else is dancing. I'm not really sure this is that type of event." I look to Blake for assistance, but he just gives me a grin and waves me on.

"Nonsense. This is my gala, and if I want to dance, I'll bloody well dance." His feet move back and forth in a two-step while his hips gyrate. "Life's too short to worry about what other people are doing, my dear." He starts shimmying around me. "Now, are you going to just stand back and watch, or are you going to step up and live?" The way he waggles his bushy eyebrows at me makes it impossible to say no.

"Oh, what the hell." I shrug, shoving my glass onto a nearby table. I lift the skirt of my dress and proceed to boogie on down with Frank.

Looking at him busting moves in the middle of a crowded banquet hall, it's hard to imagine this is the same man who'd been put down and ridiculed for his beliefs. That anyone could want to beat him to within an inch of his life doesn't bear thinking about. And yet, through all his adversity, he still holds onto the belief that ultimately, people are good.

I find myself taking on some of that philosophy as I notice people gathering around our impromptu dance off. He's quite the fancy-foot, and it doesn't take long for the crowd to build. Some smile, raising their glasses in a toast, some whisper behind their hands, no doubt discussing how inebriated I must be, but I don't care. For once I'm having fun without being under the influence. It's been a long time since I've felt this free. Perhaps Frank is onto something. To hell with what others are doing, it's time to live!

Chapter twelve

"And this, my dear, is the lovely Genevieve." Frank's hand leaves the small of my back to take Genevieve's. Much like he did when he met me, he plants a soft kiss on the back of her hand, his lips lingering a touch longer. "Genevieve, this is Emma." His eyes never leave hers as he speaks.

"It's a pleasure," she says, holding her hand out to me from her wheelchair.

"Likewise."

"Genevieve is the one who got away," Frank stage whispers behind his hand. "But I'm not letting that stop me." He winks, patting her hand. "I'll win her back."

She smiles adoringly at him. "We'll see." Light dances in her eyes, and I can tell they mean a great deal to each other. It seems crazy that people so obviously in love wouldn't be together given the chance. What I wouldn't give to have a man look at me the way he looks at her. It's so intimate, as if they're communicating with just their eyes. So intimate I feel the need to step away and give them some time alone.

Spotting Blake leaning up against the bar, I make my way over to him. "Hey, stranger."

"Hey, I thought I'd lost you for the night." He chuckles, nodding towards Frank. "He's something else, right?"

I follow his gaze. "He sure is. Such a lust for life." I grin. "And Genevieve too, it would seem. What's their deal anyway? Why aren't they together?"

"They were once. A little over a year after they started seeing each other, she developed symptoms of ALS."

My hand flies to my chest. "But that's life threatening, isn't it? Where your body just gives out?"

He nods. "Yeah. It started in her hands and arms, then her feet, hence the chair."

I watch as Frank brushes a hair from her face, cupping her chin. He leans in close, whispering something that makes her smile. I couldn't imagine he would abandon her in her time of need.

"She asked him to leave?"

He nods. "She did. She didn't want to be a burden on him, so she told him to go and live the life she couldn't." He stares off into the distance. "He argued that it wasn't living if he wasn't with the woman he loved, but she told him it was what she wanted, and he'd do just about anything for her."

We sit in silence, me watching Frank wheel Genevieve around the room, and Blake staring into the bottom of his glass.

"So, who is she?" I ask, nudging his arm with mine.

He looks up. "Who?"

"The one on your mind." He shakes his head with a light laugh. "Come on, you can tell me." I pull my fingers across my lips. "I won't tell a soul." He gives me a side eye which I choose to ignore, instead, scanning the room for a potential love interest of his. Spying a beautiful red-head in an emerald-green frock, I point. "Is it her?" The look in his eyes tells me I'm way off. "Hmmm."

"You can look, but you'll never find what you're looking for." He grins, bringing his glass to his lips, and as he does, his eyes flit up. When I follow his gaze, I see a tall, dark-haired man staring heatedly at Blake. It takes me a minute to realize he's the camera man from the other day.

I click my tongue. "He certainly scrubs up well."

Blake's head whips around to face me, a slight color to his already golden complexion. "What?"

"It's nothing to be ashamed of."

"I don't know what you're talking about." His eyes fall back to his glass before he slugs it back.

I place my hand on his arm. "You do." I run my hand up his chest to straighten his tie. "Now, maybe, you should take a leaf out of Frank's book, and go live the life you want."

"It's not that simple."

"Then simplify it. Anyone with half a brain can see how you look at each other. What's stopping you?"

"Blake!" Bo walks up, slapping a hand on his brother's shoulder. A look of shame crosses Blake's face, and it becomes crystal clear why he can't be true to himself. "And if it isn't your latest muse." He grins at me. "I didn't know we were dating the cast now."

"We're n—"

"Honey," I interrupt. "It's okay, we can tell Bo." Blake looks at me in confusion. "I know I said I'd rather keep it quiet so the others don't think I'm getting special treatment, but, he's your brother." I smile sweetly, hoping he'll follow my lead.

"Oh, right." He brings his hand up to rest on the small of my back. "It's still early days."

"You sly dog!" He waves the bartender over. "A round of drinks, good sir. We're celebrating! My brother's finally got himself a woman."

I inwardly cringe, realizing just how 'simple' it would be for Blake to come forward if his own brother acts this way. No wonder he keeps it under wraps.

"What are you doing?" he whispers in my ear.

"Trying to help you."

"Aww, look at you two, whispering sweet nothings like love birds." Bo smirks, handing us a shot of vodka each. "To newfound love and keeping secrets." He winks, downing the drink in one go. "Though, you do realize you're out in public, right?"

"We're also working on a project together. I think that gives us reason to be attending a gala, don't you?" I hand my empty shot glass back to him with a raised brow, almost challenging him to disagree.

Instead, he turns to Blake with a grin. "She's feisty. I like her."

"Your approval means a lot to me, brother." Blake's voice is dripping with sarcasm, but I can tell underneath it, he really means what he said. "And what about you?" He holds his arm out wide, searching the room. "It's not like you to show up empty-handed."

A fleeting look of hurt crosses his face before he grins to cover it up. "Why limit myself to just one when I can have my pick." He waves his arm around the room in a cocky gesture of masculinity.

"Don't forget to pee in the corner and mark your territory."

"Oooh." He flings a hand to his heart, stumbling backwards. "Did you just call me a bitch?"

I shrug. "If the shoe fits."

His eyes flick between mine before a slow smile curls his lips and he belts out a laugh. "Seriously, Blake. This one's a keeper."

***

The ride back to my house is a quiet one. To say the evening was an eye-opener is an understatement. Not only did I meet one of the most ebullient men I've ever come across, but I discovered another piece to the puzzle that is Blake Ramirez. I can understand how he came to produce a movie such as *All about Frank*, but the question begs to be answered, why not follow in his footsteps and be true to himself?

Granted, I've never had to worry about how my parents would react to my sexual preferences. As far as I'm concerned, it's none of their business who I choose to fornicate with, but if I was to flaunt a woman in their faces, they wouldn't think any less of me. I get the feeling it's not quite the same for Blake and his family. No doubt the untouchable Marty Ramirez would have a thing or two to say about how his son chooses to spend his time, or more importantly, who he's spending it with.

Blake's silence has me questioning whether what I did was the right thing to do. I can't tell if he's mad at me, or just deep in thought—we only met each other a few days ago, after all. Perhaps me jumping in to rescue him wasn't the wisest of moves.

"I'm sorry if that was inappropriate back there." I swivel in my seat. "It just kinda came out."

"It's okay." He smiles, reaching over to grab my hand. "I'm not mad. In fact, I'm quite the opposite."

"You are?"

"Yeah." He nods. "I've been thinking. And it's totally fine for you to say no, okay? This isn't going to affect your job with the studio in any way."

"Okay." I draw the word out, intrigued to hear his proposition.

"I just thought that maybe, for now at least, you and I could... Be seen to be a couple?" He shifts in his seat. "Only as a front. I'm not asking you to do anything... untoward."

"I see. And where does Javier fit into this?"

"The same place he's been for the past five months. By my side."

"Just not in public."

He sighs, rubbing his forehead with his thumb and forefinger. "Yes. I know it sounds like he's my dirty little secret, but I'm not ready to come out yet, okay?"

"Well, you might want to tone down the eye-fucking then, because from where I was standing, it was clear as day. I don't know how no one else has noticed."

"We'll be more discreet. It's hard when we can't be together."

"I bet it is." I snort.

"You know what I mean. Look, I promise, I'll tell Bo soon, and my father."

"I'm going to stop you right there." I grab his other hand, pulling him closer. "You don't have to explain yourself to me. I was being an ass. It's your life, and if I've learned anything from Frank, it's that you've gotta live it your way. If that means we become a fake couple, then so be it."

His shoulders slump, and he exhales a long slow breath. "Thank you. You have no idea what this means to me."

"Aww, honey, you know I'm just using you, right? To get my rep back?" I toss him a wink as I open the door.

He throws his head back in a boisterous laugh. "You know, if this fake relationship doesn't work out, you'd be perfect for my brother."

"He wishes." I step out into the cool night. "Goodnight, Blake."

"Night, Emma."

Chapter thirteen

"Are you trying to give me a heart attack?" Cybil's harsh voice permeates my dreams and I slowly blink my eyes open.

I really need to get that key off her.

"To what do I owe this pleasure?" I push myself up to a sitting position before swinging my legs out of bed.

Cybil eyes me warily, a paper held firm in her clutch. "Did you *do* anything last night?" She lifts a brow, pursing her lips.

"Yeah, actually. I went to a gala evening with Blake. Why?" I rack my brains for something I may have done to embarrass myself once again but come up empty. I'd had a great time, with limited booze, I might add. Nothing untoward happened to my knowledge.

"This ring any bells?" She holds the paper out to me, and there, right on the front page, is a picture of me knocking back a glass of wine. To the right of that is an image of me mid-dance with

Frank, my head thrown back in laughter, my skirt hitched above my knees. The caption reads *"Jones at it again".*

A strangled laugh falls from my lips. "This is taken out of context. I wasn't drunk. I was just having a bit of fun."

"I'm well aware of your type of fun."

"I'm serious, Cybil. Ask Blake. I only had three drinks the entire night."

"Someone who sits on three drinks the entire night, doesn't swallow the whole glass in one go." She taps her foot impatiently. "The evidence is right there in black and white."

"Come on, Cybil. You said yourself, they're vultures who will twist anything to get a story. That's what this is. And I bet I know who it was too."

She quirks an eyebrow, folding her arms across her chest. "I'm listening."

"When we arrived, there was this one reporter who singled me out, asking about my family history." I lift my gaze to meet hers. "I froze, but Blake stepped in and told him to have some respect. I'd bet almost anything it was him who did this."

"Your assumption is probably right. However, that still doesn't help with your credibility. You have to be more careful. You can't be seen with a drink in your hand right now. It's not good for your image."

"Well that's going to be tricky when the character I'm playing in Blake's movie is a drunk."

She pinches the bridge of her nose, closing her eyes. "Can you at least try to keep it to a dull roar when you're out in public? If you must drink, do it in the comfort of your own home."

Reaching up, I pull her hand from her face. Her body stiffens at the contact, but I don't move my hand. "I promise you. I wasn't drunk last night, and I'll do my best to be the perfect little actress you want me to be." The look in her eyes tells me she doesn't fully believe me. I wave a hand up and down my body. "Look at me. Do I look like I was hitting the juice hard last night?"

She cocks her head to the side. "No. I guess not."

"You sure now? I can walk a straight line for you. Sing the alphabet backwards. No, probably not that." I snort. "Look, I can even touch my nose without any effort." I hold my arms out wide, then bring a finger to the tip of my nose, one at a time. "Sober as a judge, your honor."

She holds a hand up to stop me. "Just... Be more careful, that's all I'm saying. Too many of these," she waves the paper in the air, "and you'll struggle to find work."

"Cross my heart and hope to die, I'll drink no more in the public eye." I make a crude cross symbol across my chest, and Cybil rolls her eyes at me.

"Why do I even bother?" she says under her breath. Folding the paper under her arm, she strides towards the door, calling out over her shoulder, "Learn your lines. Shooting starts in a few days."

"Already on it." I salute her back and grab my bath robe from its hanger. Slipping my arms through the silky sleeves, I wander through to the kitchen to make a coffee. A bottle of Irish whiskey takes pride of place in my newly filled liquor cabinet. I bought it specially to make liqueur coffees, so I can get my hit without it seeming like I'm always on it. *How's that for a dull roar?*

With my coffee pot whistling away, I open the whiskey and take a whiff. "Ah, the smell of liberation." A healthy slosh goes into the steaming coffee mug, and I'm already off to a good start. I'm going to nail my lines today. I can feel it.

I settle into the cushy pillows of my window seat, puffing them up behind my back for extra support. Blowing the steam from my coffee, I take that first sip of the day. The one that invigorates and sustains. There really is something magical about the humble coffee bean. Or perhaps it's the whiskey. Either way, I'm feeling good.

Having already skimmed the script yesterday, I skip the first few pages and dive straight in to my first lines. The plan is to have at least a third of my scenes committed to memory before lunch, which, according to the clock on the wall, gives me two hours. I could be over reaching here, but it's important to have goals.

***

Three Irish coffees later, I come up for air. Those two hours shot by so fast, but I think I've managed to at least memorize half of the third I had planned on. What's that, like a sixth? I don't know, I was never really any good at math. Still, it's more than I did yesterday, so I'm taking that as a win.

Setting my empty cup down, I stretch my arms above my head and twist my neck side-to-side to ease the tense muscles. Perhaps a walk in the garden would do my eyes and body some good. Loosen up a bit before I start going back over the script.

I pull my robe closed and secure it around my waist before slipping on some ballet flats and heading out the door. The once overgrown bush by the pool catches my eye, and I find myself walking along the edge, running my fingers across the soft leaves. It seems Brock really knows what he's doing with a pair of garden shears. Gone are the barbs and berries, leaving only vibrant green leaves.

My eyes wander across the rest of the garden that I'm ashamed to say I've let go to ruins. Brock must've been mortified to see how I'd let the place go from the pristine landscaping that adorned the place when I moved in all those months ago. It's a sad state of affairs really. The lawns are overgrown, my roses have taken on a life of their own, and I can't even see the path anymore. I'm surprised Brock didn't have a heart attack right then and there.

No. This just won't do.

With my mind made up, I storm into the garage and rummage about for something I can use to at least start making the place look respectable. I'm sure there was a cupboard of things left by the previous owner. Surely I have a trowel or whatever you use to garden with in here?

"Aha!" I hold a shiny pair of garden shears in the air. So shiny, in fact, I doubt they've ever been used in a garden. Perhaps they were ornamental. Either way, they'll do the job, I'm sure.

Deciding that a nightgown and robe aren't suitable gardening attire, I head back in to quickly change, and grab a drink for sustenance. I'm all coffeed out, but a vodka tonic will do the trick. A bit of ice and a bendy straw make for the perfect outdoor refreshment. Hell, I might even add a sprig of mint if I can find it amongst the roses.

With a floppy hat and oversized sunglasses, I stroll over to the shrubbery. My tongue chases the bendy straw around the glass until I manage to catch it and slurp in the cool liquid. Having never done any kind of gardening in my life, I'm at a loss as to where to start, so I stare at the plants hoping for divine inspiration to hit. In a way, I guess it does. In the form of a tennis ball to the noggin.

"Hey!" Vodka spills over my hands as I jerk backwards from the shock. "Ugh, gross." I give my hands a shake before licking up what's left. Waste not, want not.

The offending ball sits precariously in amongst the thorns of one of my rose bushes; of course, it would be too easy for it to have rolled softly to a stop by my feet. Using my shears, I pluck the ball from its perch, careful not to snip it in half. I suppose I should do the neighborly thing and return it, but I'm not willing to step out onto the pavement in this getup. Instead, I eye the hedge-covered concrete block wall in front of me. I can lob it over there, no sweat. I played badminton in my high school years, after all. That counts as a ball sport, of sorts.

Swinging my arm back and lifting my leg like a baseball pitcher, I hurl the ball into the air. Before I've even lifted my gaze to see where it went, I hear the unmistakeable sound of a ball hitting something hard and bouncing back. I duck just before it hits me again.

"Son of a bitch!" The ball sits on the grass by my feet, taunting me. I pick it up and throw with all my might. Aiming over the fence instead of straight up would have been a better idea, because it quickly plummets down to earth, landing with a soft thud. "Stupid ball!" I swing my leg back to kick it, but barely skim the top and fall flat on my ass. "Goddamn it! What kind of voodoo is this?"

A quiet chuckle comes from behind me, and a shadow is cast over my face as Brock peers into my eyes. "Need a little help there?" He offers his hands, pulling me to my feet in one smooth motion.

Flustered, I brush myself off. "Thank you."

"You're welcome."

"I swear, I'm not usually so accident prone. You just keep finding me on off days." A giggle slips out and I silently curse myself for allowing that to happen. Again. What is it about this guy that brings out the inner girly-girl in me?

"You seem like quite a capable woman from where I'm standing." He bends down to retrieve the ball, and I watch the muscles in his back move. *Oh to be the shirt on his back.*

"Emma?"

Shit, what did he just say? "I'm sorry, what?"

There it is again, that chuckle. There's something so charming about the sound. It's deep and almost musical, as if he's singing his joy to the world.

"What do you think?"

Son of a bitch! I did it again!

"One more time again please?" I say sweetly, forcing myself to pay close attention to his lips and the words that come from them.

He runs his hand through his hair with a grin. "Uh, I said, I've got some time to spare this afternoon if you'd like me to tidy up some of this for you." He waves at the garden. "Saves you having to dirty yourself up."

"Oh, um, sure. That would be great." I smile up at him. "But, I insist on paying you this time."

My hand grips his forearm, and I bat my lashes. "Please."

"It's really no bother. I enjoy doing it."

"All the same, I can't have you slaving away over here without any kind of reparation. If you won't take payment, at least have dinner with me?"

"Well now, I can hardly turn down the offer of a homecooked meal. I would be honored to join you."

Homecooked? No one said anything about homecooked. I hope he likes toast, because that's about all I can manage without burning the house down.

"Excellent! It's settled then."

"I'll just finish up over there and then I'm all yours." He winks, trotting away before I can say anything in return.

I turn back to the untouched roses. "Job well done, I say." Picking up my discarded shears, I traipse back to the house to Google how to make a homecooked meal.

Chapter fourteen

After searching the internet for an easy homecooked meal and then realizing I have no ingredients to make a complete dish, I throw caution to the wind and decide to brave the store down the road. With my oversized sunnies and floppy hat masking my face, I march the short distance with my head held high, hoping the confidence in my step will dissuade anyone from thinking I'm a celebrity; after all, what celebrity in their right mind would be seen walking so brazenly down the street when they should be lying low?

The store is quiet. One cashier stands idly behind her register, chewing gum and flicking through a magazine, while another sweeps the same spot over and over in some sort of a daze by the fruit and vegetables. I bypass her and head straight for the meat section. A man of Brock's stature is surely after a thick cut of steak. I carefully select the biggest piece of chuck steak I can find and throw it in the basket along with a bottle of red wine; you've got to have a drink to match the meat, or so I'm told. A prepacked salad in a plastic pottle catches my eye on the way to the counter, so I add that to the mix too.

"Paper or plastic?" the cashier asks in a bored tone. He doesn't even look me in the eye, which suits me just fine.

I try to mask my voice by lowering it an octave. "Paper, thanks." A group of giggling teenage girls enter behind me, and my heartrate picks up, hoping they won't notice me here.

"That'll be twenty-three dollars." I throw a fifty at the kid, grab my bag and make a quick getaway. Practically powerwalking down the road, I keep checking behind me, waiting for someone to recognize me, but it doesn't happen. For once, I get off scot-free.

Flinging the bag on the counter, I shrug out of my coat, hat and glasses, then set about preparing the food. I pour a glass of red to drink while I cook. The salad goes into the bowl relatively unscathed, and I even manage to mix in the dressing without too much hassle. I don't know what I was so worried about. Cooking is easy!

With the pan on the stove, I check Google again to make sure I don't overcook the steak. A few minutes on each side is all it should take according to the recipe. I crank the temperature up to high and wait for it to get hot before adding the hunk of meat. It seems to be smoking a bit, but I guess that's why there's an extraction fan above the oven. I flick the switch and watch the smoke waft up through the vents while I give the steak a prod with my finger. I'm no professional, but I think that feels about right. Time to turn it. I rummage through the drawer for a spatula or something I can use to pry the meat from the bottom of the pan but come up empty. I guess two forks will work just as well. Wedging one under each end, I stick my tongue out for concentration, then ever so carefully lift. Lift is perhaps too strong a word. What I do is more of a nudge, because the meat appears to have adhered to the pan. Non-stick my ass!

Here's a fun fact. Non-stick pans have a Teflon coating that does not go well with the scraping prongs of a fork. No, all that seems to do is gouge lines through the bottom of the pan, leaving a dusting of Teflon flavor over the meat. Tasty.

So now I have a hunk of inedible meat to serve Brock as a thank you, and I still can't get it off the damn pan. With one final shove, I wedge the fork underneath and push.

"Emma?" Brock's voice catches me off guard, and I let out a squeak as the meat comes free with my sudden movement and flies over my shoulder. "Woah!" He jumps out of the way with a chuckle.

I spin, one hand clutched to my chest and the other wielding the fork. I can just make out his face through the haze of smoke from the still-burning pan. I cough, waving a hand in front of me.

"Sorry, I didn't mean to barge in. I knocked, but there was no answer and the door was open..."

"Oh, ah... It's fine." I force a smile on my face and drop the fork to my side. My eyes flick to the half-raw, half-burned-to-a-crisp piece of meat on the floor. "Um, I might just order a pizza."

Brock bends and scoops it from the floor. "You have an interesting style of cooking." He smirks, and I hold my hands up in the air.

"Okay, you got me. I have no idea what I'm doing in the kitchen other than mixing drinks. I'd probably burn boiled water." I laugh, taking the steak from his hands and dropping it in the waste basket before opening a window for some fresh air.

"Give yourself more credit. I'm sure you could whip something up with a little guidance." He leans his hip against the counter, folding his arms across his broad chest. "I happen to be a good teacher. Why don't we make something together?"

"Oh, I don't know about that. I doubt I even have enough ingredients to make anything of substance. And this was meant to be my way of paying you back, not you helping me out of a bind again." Pinching the bridge of my nose, I shake my head. "I'm really not making a good impression here."

"Emma?" He takes my hands in his and dips his head to meet my gaze. I struggle to hold eye contact while his hands are entwined with mine, but I try to concentrate on his words. "It's really no bother. I enjoy doing these things for you. I wouldn't offer if I didn't."

"But—" He stops me with a finger to my lips, and it takes all my willpower not to lick him.

"No buts. Come on, let's see what you've got in these cupboards." The first one he opens holds a box of Frosted Flakes, a tin of pumpkin puree, a half-eaten pack of Twizzlers and two cartons of Pop-Tarts. He turns to look at me, and I shrug.

"I have a sweet tooth."

The next cupboard is equally as bare. In fact, the only one with any amount of anything is the liquor cabinet.

"I told you. I don't have much of anything. I usually order in." My tone is apologetic. "We still have salad." I hold the bowl up. "There may even be some chicken nuggets in the freezer if we're lucky. I think I bought them after watching an episode of Bobby Flay and thinking I could be the next top chef."

His eyes light up. "I haven't had chicken nuggets since I was a kid. They're perfect."

"I wouldn't go that far." I rummage through the top drawer of my freezer to find what I'm looking for. "Aha!" Beaming, I hand the box over. "Now what?"

He chuckles, shaking his head. "Now, you turn on the oven and we put them on a tray."

"If you say so." I trail a hand across the top of the oven, cooing, "I'm not wearing any panties."

"Uh." Brock clears his throat, his eyebrows almost lifting clear off his face. "Okay?"

"What? I've never had to turn on a kitchen appliance before. I don't know what they're into." I snort, then quickly cover my mouth with my hand. "Pretend you didn't hear that, again."

His laugh is deep and booming, vibrating through me. It's a sound I could listen to all day, every day, and I make it my mission to get him to laugh more often. Even if it's at my own expense.

"All right, hand 'em over. Let's see if I can pull this meal together and redeem myself." I swipe the pack from his hands and dump them on a tray then turn to him with a quirk of my brow. He nods his approval, so I slide the tray into the oven and dust my hands down my thighs. "Easy peasy. Wine?"

He eyes my already empty glass. "I can't leave a lady to drink by herself now, can I?" He reaches into the cupboard behind me for a glass and his shirt rides up giving me the perfect view of his washboard abs and that delectable V. The way his clothes cling to his form, I knew he'd be ripped, but seeing it in the flesh is a whole other thing. I catch my bottom lip with my teeth and a moan slips out.

Brock freezes, his eyes darting to mine as I clear my throat to cover my indiscretion. I finger the hem of his shirt. "This is nice. It really shows off your physique." Because that's not pervy at all.

My hands have a mind of their own, stroking from his chest down to the top of his jeans and back again. He appears to be frozen to the spot like a deer in headlights, one arm extended above me. I should stop, but I can't. I just keep stroking him like he's a fur coat. From what I can tell, there's not an ounce of fat on this man. Not one little ounce. I wonder what that's like? To have no fat whatsoever. Nothing jiggling about when you move, no muffin top hanging over your jeans. It must be nice. It's a pity I like pizza and vodka so much, or I'd seriously consider getting into better shape. All I can say is, thank Christ for Spanx!

Brock seems to come out of his daze while I'm thinking about my waistline, and slowly lowers his arm. With his shirt now firmly covering his torso, I drop my hands, embarrassed by my carry on.

"How about that wine?" His voice is husky, and damn if it isn't the sexiest thing I've ever heard in my life.

"Mmhmm," I murmur, reaching back for the bottle. I should know by now to watch what I'm doing when Brock is around, because my clumsy fingers knock the bottle, and it begins a slow, spinning dance close to the edge of the counter. Thankfully, Brock has the reflexes of a cat and grabs it before it topples to the ground. "You know, you are really handy to have around. Is there a Mrs Appleby?" My teeth clamp down on my bottom lip again, and my eyes flick to his ring finger to check for a tan line, all the while admonishing myself for being so forward. I don't know what's come over me tonight. I'm like a horny teenager.

"No, ma'am. Just me."

"Really? How does a man who looks like you, has impeccable manners, and skills up the wazoo not have anyone waiting at home?" I rest my back against the counter, taking a sip of my drink. "You're quite the catch from where I'm standing." *What the hell am I doing? Seriously, stop.*

He chuckles. "I'm nothing special."

"I beg to differ." My eyes travel languorously up and down his body. "You're pretty exceptional." *Where is the damn off button?*

"What about you, Miss Emma? How come I don't see any gentlemen callers over here?"

I raise an eyebrow. "You've been watching me, have you?"

"I wouldn't say watching..." He's cute when he's flustered. I reach out and place a hand on his forearm.

"Brock?"

"Mmm?"

"I was joking." *Leave it there. You don't need to take it any further.* "You can watch me whenever you like." *And you went and made it even more awkward. Good one, Emma.*

Chapter fifteen

Lying here, staring up at the ceiling, I go back over the disastrous evening to see if I could have done things differently. The answer is easy; of course I could've. Brock is a gentleman, not someone you throw yourself at. It's no wonder he ran for the door as soon as he could. What was I thinking, stroking his chest like that? I don't even know where that came from. I'm not usually so forward, but one look at those gorgeous abs and all my inhibitions disappeared, allowing my inner seductress to come out to play. Turns out her brand of seduction is a little on the awkward side having been out of action for so long.

Three years is a long time to be out of the dating game. I haven't even looked at another man since I said my goodbyes to Bradley and boarded that plane. He'd been my everything once upon a time. The yin to my yang, the Fred to my Wilma. But like so many things in life, it'd been too good to be true.

A shudder runs through my body and my eyes squeeze shut as his face dances briefly through my mind. I haven't allowed myself to think about him since I moved out here for a fresh start, but the emotions his face evokes, even now, are still so fresh, so raw. Perhaps because it's been on my mind since the gala night and the mention of *Sarah*.

My beautiful kid sister who was born for the stage. In a perfect world, it would've been her in my shoes, only she would've actually won the damn award, not tried to steal someone else's. But this is far from a perfect world, and there's no stage for her to grace where she is.

I blink back the tears that want to fall. Nope. I'm not going to do it. I'm not going to sit here and wallow over something I can't change. Sarah wouldn't want me to either. In fact, if she were here, she'd probably kick my ass out of bed and force me to go and see Brock. She'd tell me to pull up my big-girl panties and take charge of the situation. Take the bull by the horns, or something to that effect. Okay, so maybe grabbing him by the horn isn't the best idea, but I need to do something to prove I'm not the pervy weirdo I came across as last night.

I throw an arm across my eyes and let out a groan. The first guy to hold my interest for longer than thirty seconds in the last three years, and I go all strange on him, like when Monica tried to seduce Chandler with carrots, only I didn't cut off his toe. Not that I remember anyway.

The empty bottle of vodka I'd drowned my sorrows in after he left sits on my bedside cabinet, taunting me. My phone is face down beside it, and I'm suddenly hit with a feeling of foreboding.

No, no, no, no, no! Please, dear God, tell me I didn't drunk text him!

I reach a shaky hand out to slide my phone towards me. Quickly pulling it to my chest, I take a deep breath and close my eyes, as if the act alone will erase any wrongdoing. My heart pounds in my chest and the sound of blood whooshing through my veins fills my ears as I turn the screen to face me.

Me: Are you always such a gentleman?

Well, that's not so bad.

Brock: I try my best to be. A lady deserves respect. Thank you for a lovely dinner, by the way.

Me: *snort* chicken nuggets and salad does not a lovely dinner make. But you're welcome. You can toss my salad any time 😊 if you know what I mean.

Oh sweet Jesus, no!

Brock: I'm going to assume the glass of wine in your hand is to blame for that.

Me: Are you watching me again?

Brock: Lucky guess. It may also be because I can hear you singing "Like a Virgin" in your backyard.

Me: You can hear that?

Brock: I think the whole neighborhood can. You have a lovely voice.

Me: I practice in the shower. You should join me sometime.

Brock: In the shower?

Me: Mmhm. We could make beautiful music together.

Brock: That's the wine talking again. You should head inside, it's getting chilly out. Have a good night, Miss Emma.

Me: Party pooper.

I invited him to shower with me? Pushing the phone under my pillow and out of sight, I give the vodka bottle a filthy look. "I blame you for this." If he couldn't tell I was crushing on him before, he certainly knows it now. There's no coming back from this. It's too embarrassing. I guess I'll just have to sell up and move across town.

With a groan, I swing my legs over the edge of the bed and force myself to stand. The motion sends my head into a spiral as the room spins around before my eyes and my stomach threatens to empty its contents on the floor. I brace myself against the bedside cabinet, sucking deep breaths in through my nose until the spinning subsides. The pounding in my head seems to get louder with every breath I take, and I curse the vodka bottle once more.

On shaky legs, I edge my way down the hall to the bathroom for a little relief. I down some Tylenol and a large glass of water, but when I stare at myself in the mirror, the pounding only worsens until I've convinced myself I'm having a brain aneurism.

Lifting my eyes to the ceiling, then closing them because it hurts too much, I whisper a quiet prayer to God, promising I'll never drink again if he could just make the thrumming stop.

"Miss Emma?" a deep voice calls out, and the pounding comes in rapid succession. Someone's at the door. Praise the Lord! I'm not dying after all!

"Miss Emma, you in there?"

There's only one person it could be, and I'm not sure I'm ready to face him after last night. I'm in no fit state to greet anyone, let alone the gorgeous specimen of a man outside my door. I haven't even brushed my teeth yet.

"Emma? I just want to check you're okay. I don't want to have to break this door down, but I will!" *Oh my.* Those words shouldn't elicit delicious tingles to my core, but my word, they do. Brock Appleby using his bare hands to break down my door? Hell, I'd pay to see that.

The door handle rattles as I advance towards the entrance, my legs moving of their own accord. His voice is like a siren call to my ears, rendering me powerless. Before I know it, my body is pressed against the thick oak door, waiting.

The handle twists against my stomach as he tries once more to get through, but it's locked. Reaching down, I grab the key and twist, pulling the door towards me. I don't care that I'm wearing only a light chemise, or that my hair is like a bird's nest. I don't care that my makeup has smudged around my eyes, or that I've probably got terrible morning breath. I just need to see him and make sure we're okay after my debacle last night.

The door swings open slowly, then in a sudden whoosh, I'm pushed backwards, landing on the tiled floor with a thud. Brock lands beside me, his arm outstretched, catching my head before it can make contact with the ground.

"Are you okay? Did I hurt you?" He's up and resting on his elbow before I can even catch my breath. "Miss Emma?" His free hand runs down my side. "Are you hurt?"

"Well this certainly brings new meaning to falling for someone." I snigger, rolling on my side, nuzzling into his hand. "You know, you didn't have to throw yourself at me. A simple invite to coffee would suffice."

His eyes crinkle at the sides as he fights a smile. "Is that so?"

I nod against his hand, my lips brushing his palm. "Yup."

"I'll remember that for next time." My insides do a somersault. *He said next time.* By some miracle, this Adonis still wants to see me, even after finding me at my worst on more than one occasion.

"So, what's your story? You have a thing for damsels in distress?" I wave a hand down my body. "Because you seem to be adept at rescuing me."

"Just in the right place at the right time, I guess." He pushes off the floor, offering me his hands. "And you're far from a damsel in distress."

I reach up to take his hands and feel a cool breeze on my skin. Brock's face reddens as he averts his eyes.

"Ah, you've... um." He points a finger, waving it towards my chest, and when I look down, I'm mortified to discover one of the girls has popped out of the armhole of my chemise, her headlights on full beam.

"Oh my God!" My arms crash to my chest as I fling myself up to a sitting position. "I'm so sorry. I didn't mean to flash you like that. I mean, I didn't mean to flash you full stop. I mean, not unless you wanted me to, that is—"

"Miss Emma?" His hand is fanned across his brow, covering his eyes, but there's no hiding the smirk that lifts his lips.

"Yeah?"

"It's okay. It was... nice."

A huff of air forces out of my lungs as I meet his eyes. "I can't believe I showed you my boobs before we even got to first base." His head tilts back as a hearty laugh bursts forth.

"You really are something." He offers his hands again, and this time I take them without incident. "Now, how about that coffee?"

Chapter sixteen

"So, let me get this straight, your granddaddy is a multi-million-dollar business tycoon, and you're the heir to his throne?" I lean back, allowing the ornate metal chair back to cool my skin as one coffee turns into two.

"Yes, ma'am." Brock holds his hand up with a boyish grin. "Sorry, *Emma*."

"Tell me again why you don't have a handyman doing all that dirty work for you?" I peer at him over my Irish coffee, curious as to what makes this man tick.

He shrugs, rubbing a hand across his stubbled chin. "My folks owned a ranch when I was growing up, and I got used to working with my hands. There was always something needed doing on the ranch, and it didn't matter who you were, you all pitched in to help." His eyes follow a passing car before he speaks again. "When they died, I was too young to take control of the ranch, so I was brought here to live with my granddaddy. He'd like me to take over one day, but—" He shakes his head. "—It's not really my thing. The CEO knows his stuff, and I'll probably leave it up to him. I'd rather be working the land."

I lean forward, resting my hand on his. "I'm so sorry, Brock, I didn't know. How old were you... when it happened?"

"Thirteen. A drunk driver took the corner too fast, sent them careening off the road. The truck rolled twice and landed upside down in a water race."

My heart drops into my stomach and my hand flies to my mouth as I gasp. "Oh my God. That's horrible. Did they catch him? The guy who hit them?"

"They didn't have to. He died on impact. Some young kid out for a joyride with his friends after a party." He shakes his head. "They said he was three times over the legal limit. He shouldn't have been able to walk straight, let alone drive, and yet his friends jumped in the car with him." His eyes take on a faraway look as he stares across the street. "I still don't understand how anyone could let that happen." He turns to meet my gaze and it's like a shot to the heart. The pain in that look sears straight through me, and in some cruel twist of fate, it makes me want a drink more than ever. He tells me that alcohol killed his parents, and I'm sitting here with whiskey in my coffee and a craving for more.

What's wrong with me?

The intensity of his stare is too much, and I have to break it. Shuffling forward in my seat and clearing my throat, I change the subject. "And the ranch? Do you still have it?"

The darkness leaves his eyes and the corners of his mouth pull up slightly. "Yes, ma'am. Our foreman, Henry, still lives out there in his quarters. He keeps an eye on the place, keeps it running smoothly while I'm out here helping my granddaddy."

"You plan on going back there to stay then?"

"I do. The land is in my blood. It's where I'm meant to be." He speaks with such conviction, I'm almost jealous. I don't think I've ever felt for certain that I'm meant to be anywhere. Certainly not here in Hollywood. I've paid my dues, and I've worked hard to get here, but I don't feel it in my bones that this is where I should be. In fact, up until three years ago, Hollywood wasn't even on my radar. I had no plans, no idea what I wanted to do with my life. As far as I was concerned, I was destined for a quiet, mundane life. That all got flipped on its head after I found Sarah. Now I'm out here, living the life she was destined for.

I sigh wistfully. "Sounds like a great place. I'd love to see it sometime."

"I'd love to show you." He smiles, that peaceful calm back in his eyes. "It really is a sight to see. No city lights tainting the night sky, and the stars are like nothing you've ever seen."

"Sounds beautiful."

"Yeah." He leans back, linking his hands behind his neck. "What about you? What's your story?"

"Oh." I wave a hand through the air. "Not much to tell, I'm afraid."

"Come on, there's got to be a story behind you coming out here and making a name for yourself." A smirk settles on his face as he watches me. *He's done his homework. He knows who I am. I should've known he'd find out eventually.*

Covering my face with my hands, I peek through my fingers. "How much do you know?"

"Hmm, let me see." He taps a finger against his chin before chuckling. "I know you're not Emma Stone."

Oh God.

A groan escapes my lips as I try to hide behind my large coffee mug. "It was an honest mistake."

His fingers curl around my wrist, lowering the mug from in front of my face. "Emma, look at me."

I shake my head, ducking it low before dragging my eyes up to meet his. *This is it. The moment when he tells me I'm not good enough.*

"You don't ever have to hide that pretty face from me, okay?"

"Um, okay?" I draw the word out into more of a question than a statement. My brow creases as I try to work out his angle. He can't possibly be interested in me after what he just told me. Not when I've been branded an alcoholic by every man and his dog. Perhaps he wants me as a project, like a fixer-upper.

"Besides, I heard it plain as day. They said your name." He winks as his hand slides across mine until our fingers are interlaced. His thumb draws circles across my palm, sending shivers of pleasure through my body before I realize what he's just said.

"Wait, you actually saw it? Like, you watched it? You didn't just read about it in the tabloids?"

He nods. "Yes, ma'am, I did watch it."

"No offence, but you don't seem the type."

"None taken. And you're right, I'm not the type, but I'd have to be walking around with my head in the dirt not to see your face plastered on every paper." He shrugs, an easy smile forming on his lips. "You can't blame a guy for being curious."

"And you're not the least bit upset about what they've been saying about me? That doesn't bother you after what you just told me about your parents?"

Clearing his throat, he leans forward. "I'm not some country hick who doesn't see the press have their own agenda. I may know a thing or two about animals, but I'm no sheep. I form my own opinions." He pauses, his eyes drifting to our joined hands. "I'm not going to pretend it's my favorite thing about you, because it's not by a long shot. But I'm not going to judge you for it either. There's no harm in a little bit of fun. It's when it goes too far and hurts people I have an issue with it."

I swallow the lump forming in my throat, waiting for the ball to drop. He might say he's okay with it, but really, how can he be? It's only a matter of time before my past comes crashing back to haunt me, and then what? He'll want nothing to do with me.

A squeeze of my hand draws my attention back to Brock. "Whatever demons you're running from, must be pretty bad if you're needing to drown them in alcohol." My eyes flick up to meet his, my mouth falling open. "You don't hide it quite as well as you think." He sits back against the chair, a hand raised. "And I don't expect you to tell me straight away, or at all, if you don't want to. But, I'm a firm believer in second chances, and if you don't mind me saying, you seem like you could use one about now."

Tears fill my eyes as I pull back from him. Wrapping my arms around my waist, I try desperately to rein it in, not willing to cry in public and cause yet another scene. "I... um..." I shake my head, clearing my throat. "That's very nice of you to say, but you don't know what you're talking about."

His lips purse as he runs a hand across his stubbled jaw. "I'm sorry if I've overstepped. It wasn't my intention to offend."

"No. You didn't offend. Believe me, I've heard worse." I turn to look at him, this sweet man who deserves someone so much better. "But what you don't understand, is I'm not running from my demons." I tip the last of the coffee down my throat before pushing up from the table and throwing some cash down. "I *am* the demon."

Chapter seventeen

"Whoa, what's that supposed to mean?" He scoots his chair back and follows after me. "Emma?" His grip on my arm is gentle but firm. "Talk to me."

"I don't think this—" I point between the two of us, "—is going to work."

"This—" he mimics me, gesturing back and forth, "—has barely had a chance to get off the ground, and you're already pulling the pin?" His eyes search mine. "What are you afraid of?"

"You don't know anything about me. You have no idea what you're getting in to."

"No offence, Emma, but I beg to differ. I know plenty about you." He starts counting on his fingers. "I know that you're not afraid to scale a fence or get dirty. I know that you're a terrible cook and know nothing about gardening. I know that you're trying to prove something to someone, maybe yourself." He lowers his voice, stepping in close. "I know that you've been sneaking whiskey into your coffee when you don't think I'm looking."

I open my mouth to speak but he presses a finger to my lips. "I know all these things, but it's not enough to scare me away." His hand slides down my arm to my hand, bringing it to his lips. "I'm truly sorry for upsetting you, Emma. I never meant for that to happen." He places my palm over his chest. "I won't push you to talk about it, just know that these ears are good for listening if you do decide to share, and these arms will always be there to catch you if you fall." He takes a step back, his gaze holding firm. "I like you, and I'm pretty sure you like me too, but if you're not ready, that's okay. I'll walk away right now and leave you be. Just say the word."

My teeth clamp onto my bottom lip as I mull it over. There's no doubt in my mind he's too good for me, but for whatever reason, he wants to give it a shot. He wants me, flaws and all. How can I say no to that?

"I don't want you to go." The words are barely more than a whisper on the wind, but he hears me loud and clear. His lips curl up into that panty-dropping smile, and those dimples come out to play. It's impossible to resist smiling back. "I just have one condition." I hold a finger in the air.

"Name it."

"You have to knock off this whole ma'am and Miss Emma business. It's just Emma, okay? I can't date someone who addresses me like their boss."

He chuckles, nodding his head. "You're gonna have to cut me some slack on that one, but I'll do my best. It's engrained on my soul to always address a lady that way."

"Well, that's easy. Just don't think of me as a lady then."

His laughter booms as he takes hold of my hand once more. "How exactly do I think of you then? Because last time I checked, if it walks like a lady, talks like a lady, it's probably a lady."

"Oh—" I wave a hand through the air, "—I very rarely walk and talk like a lady. You'll see." I turn on my heels and start walking in a John Cleesesque way towards Betsy. "Better?"

"Mmhmm, much better," he says, casually strolling beside me as if it's the most normal thing in the world, but I can see the barely contained amusement in his eyes. He's close to breaking, and I intend on making that happen.

With my legs kicking high in the air, I add in a bob with every shift of my weight and extend my free arm into that of a bird's wing flapping. It only takes two steps before he can no longer keep it in. His cheeks puff out as his laughter forces its way free, and it's a sight to behold. This is how I always want him to be; not looking at me with concern or pity, but with joyous rapture. I want to see that boyish grin and bathe in the sea of those baby blues as they shine with amusement. But more than anything, I want to be the one to put that shine there in the first place. I want to be the one to make him smile, make him happy. And as of right now, I vow to make it happen.

Chapter eighteen

"Favorite movie?" I ask, popping a piece of popcorn in my mouth and humming. The buttery goodness is something I haven't enjoyed in forever. I always shied away from it because it reminded me of the theatre and Sarah, but with Brock, it doesn't seem quite so scary.

"That's easy. *Die Hard.*"

I laugh. "That's really your favorite?" He nods with a grin. "You're such a boy."

"Okay then, what's your favorite? It better not be anything girly like *Dirty Dancing* or *The Princess Bride.*"

I snort, and this time I don't even bother covering my mouth. "Do I look like the kind of girly girl who would be into those?"

He tilts his head. "Well... You *do* drive a pink Rolls Royce."

I slap the back of my hand across his chest. "That pink Rolls Royce has a name. I'll have you know, Betsy is a childhood dream come to fruition. Take another guess."

"Um..." He waves a hand in circles as he thinks. "I don't know. *Moulin Rouge?*"

I sigh, shaking my head. "Much to learn, you have. Girly girl, I am not."

"You're a *Star Wars* fan?"

"From way back." I waggle my eyebrows. "Han Solo can conquer my galaxy anytime."

He barks out a laugh. "You're full of surprises."

"That's the best way to be. Keeps things interesting, don't you think?"

"I can honestly say it does with you. I never know what to expect." He entwines his fingers with mine, his thumb gently stroking across my skin. Tiny sparks of excitement and happiness swirl through me until I feel as though I may burst from his touch alone. It's been a long time since I've experienced anything remotely close to this feeling of euphoria, and it's a little scary if I'm honest. He seems to know just what I need and when, like he has some sort of psychic ability or something. It's uncanny, but oh so wonderful all the same. The eighteen months of infatuation I had with Bradley doesn't even begin to compare. What I thought was love, was merely a dependence. Something I thought I needed in my life. I relied on him to show me life, and in doing so, I lost myself, and my sister.

"You have such soft skin," he says, his eyes following the trail his thumb is making.

"All the better to seduce you with." I wink, popping another piece of popcorn in my mouth.

"Is that right?"

"I'm hoping so. Is it working?" I move the bowl of popcorn to the table and reach a hand up to cup his cheek.

His voice turns husky as he softly says, "It might be."

My tongue darts out to wet my lips as I weigh up my options. Do I go for the kill, or do I wait it out and let him make the first move?

I'm not even sure who moves first, but inch by inch, our bodies gravitate towards each other until his lips are only a breath away. A warm tingle flows from my toes all the way through me, and my racing heart kicks up a notch as I stare into those deep pools of blue. I could drown in those eyes, and I'd be happy.

"Emma?" The hoarse tone sends a shiver down my spine.

"Yes?" I breathe.

"Can I kiss you?"

"Kiss, you may." I grin, and he chuckles. His hand slips behind my neck and he brings me in, brushing his lips across mine in the sweetest kiss I've ever experienced. If I were a cartoon character, I'm sure I would've slid to the floor in a puddle of mush.

He rests his forehead against mine, and I whisper the only thing I can think to say that sums up how I feel right now. "Yippee-ki-yay."

Chapter nineteen

"And, that's a wrap for today." Blake claps his hands together. "Good work, everyone. We'll pick it up with scene fifteen, bright and early tomorrow."

The lights flash on and off as the crew go through preparations for tomorrow. I stay seated on the couch, leaning my head back against the top and stretching side to side. It had been an emotional scene and I just need a moment to let it go before I head home for the night.

"Emma, you got a minute?" Blake perches on the couch beside me, his hands steepled over his knees.

"Mmhmm. What's up?" I roll my head towards him before sitting up.

"You were great today. I was right about you, you're the perfect Taylor." He smiles, though it doesn't quite reach his eyes.

"What is it then? Is everything okay?" I hook a thumb over my shoulder. "I can do another take, if you want."

"No, nothing like that. I just wondered—" He looks side to side and lowers his voice, "—If you were still okay with our little arrangement?"

I breathe a sigh of relief. "Of course. Do you need me for another fancy schmancy shindig?" The idea of going out on the town excites me more than it should, and I find myself hoping for a big-time schmooze fest. Don't get me wrong, hanging at home with Brock every night this week has been great—more than great, actually. We're still in that honeymoon stage where you want to learn everything there is to know about the other and hang on their every word, and if I'm honest, it's been easier to stave off the drinking while he's around, but after eight days straight of shooting from 5AM, I'm ready to brush off the cobwebs and let loose a little. Of course, I may also be trying to avoid another restless night where I can't sleep for thinking of what those hands of his could do to me. I've never been one to jump straight into bed with anyone, but right now, I'm suffering from a bit of blue balls or clam jam, or whatever the cool kids are calling it these days. Brock truly is the sweetest, kindest man I've ever met. A true gentleman. And by gentleman, I mean we haven't made it past first base yet. Not even close. So, a little distraction is just what I need.

"There's a dinner thing I have to go to tonight and I was hoping you would accompany me? I understand if you already have plans. I know it's short notice."

I place my hand on his arm. "Blake? I told you I'd be happy to help you out with these things. Why are you being so funny about it? I'd love to come."

"Are you sure? I, um, saw a message come through on your phone earlier. I didn't mean to snoop, it was just there in front of me." He rakes a hand through his hair. "Are you seeing someone? Because I don't want to step on any toes or make things difficult for you." His eyes flick up to where Javier is standing, pushing buttons on his camera and pretending not to watch us. "I know it's not an easy situation."

"He's not too happy about our arrangement?"

"He understands why I need to, but he's frustrated that we can't be out in the open together. He came out to his mother and sister last year, but they accepted him with open arms. And now I'm making him hide away again because of my own insecurities." He sighs. "It's hard."

"I can get that. You've gotta do what's right for you, though. If you're not ready to tell them, then he's just going to have to deal with it if he wants to be with you." I give his arm a squeeze. "Just don't make him wait too long, okay? I think you've got a good one there."

"I won't. I just need time to lay the groundwork. It's not going to go down so well with my family. Ramirez men are known to be, well, womanizers. I'm bucking the trend."

"That's kinda your thing though, right?" I nudge his arm with my shoulder. "I know who your father is, and this—" I wave my arm around the room, "—doesn't exactly fit the mold either."

He takes a moment to look around the room, inhaling deeply through his nose before chuckling. "No, I suppose you're right."

"No suppose about it, I *am* right, and you know it." I link my arm through his, scooting closer. "You just do you, okay? Forget about what anyone else thinks."

He pats my hand with a sad smile. "Easier said than done, but thanks."

"Well, if it isn't the talk of the town. What are you two kids up to?" Bo saunters in, throwing a stack of papers on Blake's chair.

"Just coordinating our outfits for tonight." I wink, nodding at the chair. "What's with the paperwork?"

"Oh, I made some notes for tomorrow. Just a few tweaks to make it really sing." He brings his fingertips to his lips and kisses them. "Nice work on that last scene, by the way. I feel an Oscar coming," he sings.

Blake clears his throat and looks pointedly at him before his jaw drops and he slaps a hand across his mouth. "Shit, sorry." He shakes his head, whistling low through his teeth. "I'll just extract my foot from my mouth." His cheeks darken as he grimaces.

"Come on. I'm a big girl. So I missed out on one this year." I shrug, pretending it doesn't still sting. "Maybe this one will be the winner." Placing my hands on my thighs, I push up from the couch.

"Well, I'd better get outta here. Gotta go make myself look pretty for schmoozing."

Blake stands, placing his hand on my lower back. "I'll pick you up at eight, okay?"

"Perfect." I grab my things and head out the door, but not before I hear the dull thud of a fist to Bo's arm as Blake reprimands him.

***

When I pull into the drive, Brock is waiting on my doorstep, a sheen of sweat across his brow and a pile of tools by his feet. I push the button to open the garage and park Betsy in her spot for the night, while trying not to conjure up images of what else would make him sweat like that. The spell this man has cast over me is really quite something. I never knew I could be such a horn dog before.

"Hey, stranger," I say as he comes to greet me with a peck on the cheek. I run a finger down his jaw, wishing it could be my tongue. "You look all *hot* and *manly*." My teeth tug on my bottom lip as I peer up at him.

He pulls his hat from his head and rakes a hand through his hair. "It *is* mighty warm out. Fancy a swim?" One eyebrow quirks up as he watches me, his eyes flicking to my lips and back again.

Could this be it? Could this be the moment we hit first base and then some?

"A quick dip couldn't hurt." I take his hand and lead him out to the pool. "I'll just get changed. Don't you disappear on me."

"I wouldn't dream of it."

I turn and hurry back through the door, but not before I hear the splash of water as Brock dives into the pool. I can't help but take a quick peek as his muscular body streamlines through the water as if he was made for it. *Is there anything this man can't do?*

In the bedroom, I rummage through the drawers in search of a swimsuit that'll have his tongue hanging out, among other things. Tucked right in the back is a teeny blue and white striped suit with cut-outs on the sides. I'm not sure what I was thinking when I purchased it, seeing as it looks about the size of my thigh, but it's the only one that doesn't look like my nana bought it for me, so I pull it out and give it a go.

With both legs in, I wrench the fabric up over my ample thighs and bottom; so far, so good. Pushing my arms through the remaining holes, I pull it up in one smooth motion, until my boobs are covered but my ass is hanging out. I take a step towards the mirror and feel it wedge itself even further between the crack, which makes for a super comfy fit—not. What I see in the mirror is less than satisfactory. And with so little fabric, there's no way I can hide my Spanx underneath either. I mean, I'm no model; in fact, I'm shorter than average height, so how anyone taller than five foot two could wear this without being cut in two is beyond me. My backside looks like two round peaches being pulled in opposite directions, and don't get me started on the front. If that's not the worst case of camel toe, I don't know what is. And then there's the cut-out bits on the side that really just look like a holding cell for the excess "skin" I have on my hips. Yeah, I'm a real catch in this getup.

With a curse under my breath, I peel the straps from my arms and watch as it takes off, rolling down my body until it settles around my hips in a thick band of fabric, squeezing tight.

"You coming in?" Brock pokes his head around the door which elicits a scream from me and a scurry to cover my bits. This wasn't quite the impression I was going for.

His eyes widen and he quickly ducks back out, apologizing profusely. "I'm so sorry. I should've knocked first."

"Don't worry about it." I laugh, secretly dying inside. "Just a wardrobe malfunction. I'll be out in a little bit."

Mortified, I quickly remove the roll of swimwear and throw it in the trash. Boardshorts and a hideous bikini top it is. I honestly don't know what I was thinking when I bought it. Perhaps a momentary lapse of judgement on my part, though I have to admit, it does make my boobs pop.

With a towel wrapped securely around my waist, I step out into the sun, my reddened cheeks hidden beneath my sunhat. I had hoped we'd at least get past first base before he saw my wobbly bits, and no, I'm not including the nip slip from a few days back. We hadn't even started dating then.

I perch on the edge of the pool, my feet dangling in the cool water. Brock swims towards me, his arms gliding through the water without so much as a ripple. He stops just in front of me, his large hands gripping the edge on either side of my thighs as he stands. Ducking his head down to look underneath the ridiculous brim of my hat, he grins.

"There you are."

"Here I am."

"You look beautiful."

An unladylike snort bursts forth and I quickly slap a hand across my mouth, shaking my head and saying the phrase that has become a regular feature in my life as of late, "You didn't hear that."

"Hear what? The birds chirping?" He brings out the big guns—those delicious dimples that somehow make him even more attractive. How he hasn't been snaffled up already is beyond me, but I count my lucky stars it was his yard I fell into and not someone else's. All he has to do is look at me with those cerulean eyes of his, and my inhibitions disappear. He's like a drug, but the good kind.

My fingers loosen the knot at my waist, and placing my hands on his broad shoulders, I ease into the water with him. His hands land on my hips, steadying me, and I'm instantly aware of the close proximity of our bodies. Our hot, wet, not-very-covered bodies. My throat goes dry as I slide my hands down his firm chest and back up to wrap around his neck. I watch as his Adam's apple bobs up and down, his eyes darting to my lips once more. My teeth find purchase, bringing my bottom lip in as I wait with bated breath.

With one fluid movement, he raises his hand to cushion my back as he presses me into the edge of the pool, a low growl leaving his lips. Pressing his forehead to mine, he closes his eyes. "I can only be expected to keep my hands off you for so long." Bringing his free hand up to cup my chin, his thumb tugs at my lips, pulling it free. "Especially when you come out here dressed like that." He stares into my eyes, as if asking for permission. I barely manage to nod before his lips collide with mine, his tongue seeking entrance.

With a whimper, I melt into his arms, my fingers snaking into his hair.

He drags his hands down to cup my ass, and I take that as an invitation to wrap my legs around his waist. I curse my decision to wear boardshorts instead of a bikini, but even through all that fabric I can feel his arousal as I rock my hips. Even with our bodies entwined, I want so much more. I *need* to be closer.

Breaking away, Brock rests his forehead against mine again, his breath coming out in pants. "You're making it very hard to not rush things, you know?"

"I can tell," I say, rubbing myself against him again. He groans, planting another kiss to my lips.

"I'm trying to be chivalrous."

"I'll let you in on a little secret. Sometimes, it's okay not to be." I give one final wiggle of my hips before unwrapping myself from his torso. "But, if that's the way you want it..."

He growls, gripping my hips and dropping his head to my shoulder. "I'm probably going to regret this, but it is." He leans back, cupping my jaw with both hands. "You deserve to be treated with respect. You're not just a quick fuck in the pool."

I gasp, my eyes widening in mock outrage. "Did you just say fuck? That kind of language is unbecoming of a gentleman."

"And a lady wouldn't climb me like a beanpole." He grins.

"Ah, that's where you're mistaken. You keep forgetting, I'm not a lady." I slip from his arms and dive into the water, across to the other side. Leaning my elbows on the ledge behind me, I watch him glide languorously towards me. "For the record, I love that you want to treat me with respect. It's a nice change."

A frown flits across his face. "You shouldn't accept anything other than that."

"Well, when you're young and don't know any better, I guess it's easy to forget that." I shrug, turning my eyes away from his penetrating gaze.

"Hey." He tilts my chin so I'm facing him again. I don't know why I brought it up. I should've known he'd want to ask questions. He must see the reluctance in my eyes though because instead, he asks, "Do you have any plans for this evening? Would you care to join me for dinner?"

"I wish I could, but I can't, sorry. I'm going to a thing with Blake tonight."

He quirks an eyebrow, leaning back. "Oh, really?"

"It's not like that. We have an... arrangement."

"Okay." He draws the word out.

"Purely platonic, I assure you."

"Emma, it's okay. I trust you." He smiles, brushing his lips gently across mine.

"It probably won't be late. Maybe we could meet up after?"

"Don't you have an early call?"

"Mmm, I do, but—" I wrap my arms around his neck, pulling him closer, "—I thought maybe I could show you how unlike a lady I really am.

Chapter twenty

"So, whose party is this, and what do I need to know?" I take a sip of the champagne Blake poured me as soon as the limo began to move.

"I wouldn't call it a party. More of a gathering. It'll be mainly other directors and producers there, with a handful of wannabes and up-and-comers."

"Right, so a pissing contest then." I nod, settling back in the plush leather seat.

Blake chuckles as he pours himself a glass. "You could say that, yes." With a glint in his eye, he raises his glass skyward. "To competition."

"To competition."

"Thank you for accompanying me on such short notice. I know you probably had other things you'd rather be doing than schmoozing stuck-up suits."

"Nothing that couldn't keep." Heat pools in my core as I recall the afternoon's antics and the promise of what might come (literally) later tonight. Just the thought of Brock's big, strong hands caressing my skin is enough to set me on fire, and I have to squeeze my thighs together just to get some relief.

"Hmm, judging by the blush coloring your cheeks, I'm not sure I believe you, but I appreciate it all the same." Leaning forward, he places a hand on my knee. "If there's ever anything you need, you have only to ask. I know this isn't the most conventional of business relationships we've got going here, and I'm asking far beyond what any director should ask his cast."

"Come now, Blake. I'd like to think we've moved past the director and cast member status to friends." Flicking my hair over my shoulder, I pull out a bit of Valley Girl lingo. "Like, I mean, I am like your pretend girlfriend, after all."

With a shake of his head, Blake rests back in his seat, chuckling. "There's no one quite like you, Emma."

"Yeah, they broke the mold with me. You can't beat perfection." I extend my arm, opening my hand in a 'mic drop' gesture.

The limo slows, pulling up a long drive that winds around a circular fountain complete with a carving of a naked man in the center. He stands rather proudly, with hands on hips and a smirk on his face, almost as if he's gloating over what he's packing, which, I might add, is a rather hefty bulge.

I can't help letting out a whistle as I admire his stature. "Wow. Now that is a conversation starter."

"Wait until you meet the man himself."

My eyes bug out, and I nearly choke on my champagne. "Excuse me?" I point at the chiseled stone. "That's an actual sculpture of someone here?"

Blake scoffs. "He'd like to think so. The real thing isn't quite so... grandiose, I assure you."

I lean back with a quirk of my brow. "Ooh you speaking from personal experience? Or do you have it on good authority? Come on, dish the dirt."

He steps out of the car, offering his hand with a flourish. "I couldn't possibly reveal my sources. I am a gentleman, after all."

Pursing my lips, I look him up and down before nodding. "Mmhmm. Something tells me you haven't shaken hands with the snake, so I'll assume it was someone you know and trust who spilled the beans."

"Shaken hands with the snake? You certainly have a way with words. And you're not far off base either, I might add." He glances up at the statue, his lips forming a straight line. "He's most definitely got serpent qualities, and not in the good way."

"Wow, sounds like quite a catch." I roll my eyes. "Why are we even here if you don't like the guy?"

"You've been around a while now, you should know it's all about who you know, not what you know in this business."

"And dealing with a dastardly snake is beneficial?" I can't hide the scepticism in my voice. I don't care who his family is, you don't go into business with people you can't trust, and from what I'm gathering, this guy is far from trustworthy.

"Sometimes it's a necessary evil, I'm afraid. Better the devil you know and all that."

The doors swing open as we approach, and I can't help thinking what a crappy job that must be; constantly watching for people to open the door before they have to knock. Probably some poor fool who thinks it'll be his big break into Hollywood and all its glory.

We enter a vast foyer filled with suits and broads. In the center is a rather large bust of our host, and behind, a sprawling staircase leading up to the next floor.

"Certainly rates himself, doesn't he?" I whisper behind my hand, all the while keeping a smile plastered on my face as I nod to the passers-by.

"That he does."

Blake escorts me around the room, introducing me to everyone, though I'm not sure it's necessary. I can tell by the smirks on their faces, they know who I am and what I did. I don't think I'll ever be able to live down the day I tried to steal Emma Stone's Oscar. But, on the positive side, at least if they didn't already, they definitely know who I am now. I don't think it matters how they heard of me, just that I'm now on their radar, and who knows? Perhaps I might fit the bill for one of their upcoming productions. Hell, if the Ramirez brothers are willing to take a chance on me, surely others will follow suit.

Swiping a glass of champagne off a passing tray, I fake laugh as I'm reminded once again of my mishap by the lady in front of us, as if I wasn't actually there experiencing it first-hand. "And the look on your face!" She laughs, dabbing a napkin beneath her eyes. "Priceless!"

Blake squeezes my hand, changing the subject to discuss the movie we're working on together when a meaty hand slaps his shoulder, interrupting us.

"Blake! Glad you could make it." He thrusts his hand out for Blake to shake, his eyes raking over my body hungrily. "You've been holding out on me, it would seem. Who is this fine-looking specimen?" Blake smiles, his hand landing on my lower back and pulling me in to his side possessively. I don't miss the change in his eyes or the fact his body is practically pulsing with tension, which can mean only one thing. The serpent is upon us.

"Tony, how are you?" They shake hands, and I try not to let my jaw drop as I realize just who this is. He's a Hollywood legend, one I never imagined would get Blake so riled up.

But two seconds in his presence and I begin to get an inkling as to the animosity. Tony, though speaking to Blake, can't seem to take his eyes off me. To say I'm uncomfortable is an understatement. His beady eyes seem to be undressing me, and it takes everything in me not to shudder under his watchful gaze.

Blake clears his throat. "Tony, this is Emma Jones. Emma, Tony Bradford." Tony takes my hand in his, bringing it to his lips. I fight the urge to pull away, knowing this is important to Blake.

"Miss Jones, what a pleasure to meet you." He winks, standing up to his full height. "Why does that name sound so familiar?"

Here we go.

"She's my new leading lady, that's why." Blake jumps to my rescue. "One heck of a woman, and a fine actress to boot." He tightens his grip on me, turning to face me with a look of pure pride.

"I certainly wouldn't boot her anywhere. Not unless it was out of my bed to finish her on the floor." Tony barks out a laugh, and Blake bristles beside me.

I know men talk crudely about women in the locker room, hell, I know women who can be just as crass about men, but hearing it spoken out loud, in public, about me? That's a whole other kettle of fish. I don't even know how to respond, so I do what I always do. Use humor.

"I think you're doing it wrong if you need to boot her out of bed to get her to finish. You ever heard of foreplay? Look it up. It's all the rage these days." I waggle my eyebrows before tipping my glass back and inhaling the liquid. If this is what the night has instore, I'm going to need a lot more where that came from.

Tony stares for a beat, perhaps unsure what to make of me. He glances at Blake, who looks as though he's struggling to contain his mirth, then tips his head back, roaring with laughter as he slaps a hand on Blake's shoulder once more.

He shakes a finger at me, still chuckling to himself. "You'll have to keep your eyes on this one, I think."

Blake gives my hip a squeeze. "Don't I know it."

***

"Brock? Broooooock?" I whisper-sing as I stumble through the front door and down the hallway. It's a little after midnight; a tad later than anticipated, but I'm still hoping he stayed and waited. Our little escapade in the pool this afternoon got me all hot and bothered, and the more alcohol I consumed to take my mind off it, the more I wanted to get home to see him.

"Brock? You awake?" I reach the door to my room and strike what I hope is a sexy pose.

"Emma?" His voice is deep and husky, and just the sound alone is enough to make me squirm on the spot.

"Hey," I say, trying to sound sultry. "Did you miss me?" I reach down to pull my heels off and toss them across the floor.

"I always do." There's a rustling sound as he sweeps the covers back and drags himself up the bed to sit. The tiny sliver of light shining through the drapes casts a glow on his bare chest, and I'm struck speechless. Suddenly I'm no longer intoxicated with alcohol, but with the man before me. How is this Adonis here with me? He belongs on the back of a horse, corralling cattle, or whatever it is cowboys do.

"Emma?"

"Mmm?"

"Everything okay?"

"Mmmhmmm." I can barely think straight, let alone form a coherent answer. Ever since I fell into his arms, I've dreamt of this moment, but now that it's here, I'm rendered immobile. My brain and body don't seem to want to cooperate with each other, and the longer I stand here staring at him, the more he's going to think I'm some freak who can't function like a normal human being.

Dragging my eyes away from his body, I force myself to take a step forward. One foot in front of the other, nice and slow. I keep my eyes cast down so as not to be distracted by his beauty, so when his hand reaches out and caresses my cheek, I almost jump out of my skin.

"Jesus!" My hand flies to my chest as a nervous giggle bubbles up. "You'll give a girl a heart attack if you go sneaking around like that."

He chuckles. "I didn't realize I was sneaking."

"Maybe I just didn't hear you over my heart pounding." I swallow, my throat suddenly feeling as dry as the Sahara. "I need a drink. Be right back." Turning on my heels, I dart back down the hallway and out to the kitchen to my secret stash. I don't know why I'm so nervous when this afternoon I practically threw myself at him, but I'm shaking like a leaf.

Unscrewing the cap, I lift the vodka bottle to my lips and take a deep pull of liquid courage. *You can do this.*

With shaky fingers, I grip the hem of my dress and pull it over my head, letting it fall to the ground behind me as I stalk back to the bedroom with a newfound confidence. I pause in the doorway, hearing the audible intake of breath as Brock lays eyes on me in black lace panties and bra and nothing else.

"Emma." The husky tone to his voice as he breathes my name sends a jolt straight to my core. I've never wanted a man as much as I want him right now.

With our eyes locked, we meet in the middle like two magnets drawn to each other. His hands cup my face as I run my arms around his waist. His lips brush mine ever so lightly before he pulls back, his eyes searching mine.

"You've been drinking." It's not a question, but a statement. One filled with disappointment.

"I, um..." *have no excuse. God, how could I be so stupid?*

Leaning his forehead to mine, he groans. "We can't do this, Emma. Not now."

"What? What do you mean?" A sinking feeling hits the pit of my stomach as I brace myself for the inevitable; he's realized I'm not good enough for him.

"This." He points a finger back and forth between us. "How do I know this is what you want and not just because you're drunk?"

A wave of relief washes over me as I realize he isn't ending it. Peering up at him, I try to keep my voice level and sober-sounding. "I'm not so drunk I don't know what I want, and what I want is you." I push up onto my tiptoes and press my lips to his.

"I won't take advantage of you. That's not how I was raised."

"Brock, I promise you, you're not taking advantage. I want this. I want you."

He pulls back, his eyes flicking between mine. "Are you *sure* this is what you want?"

"I've never been more sure of anything in my life." I don't let him say anything else, crushing my lips to his, showing him just how much I need him. He resists for only a second before wrapping his arms around me and pulling me against his chest. A low groan rumbles through him as I run my tongue along the seam of his lips.

Breaking from the kiss, he lifts me in his arms as if I weigh no more than a feather and carries me to the bed. "You'll be the death of me, Emma," he whispers hoarsely, laying me down and settling between my thighs which remain wrapped firmly around his waist. He rests his elbows on either side of my head, gently caressing my face as he feathers kisses along my jaw and down my throat. For someone so big and strong, he has the lightest of touches. So gentle, as if he's afraid he'll break me.

I twine my fingers through his hair, bringing his lips back to mine. His bare chest is pressed against me, but even with only my bra between us, it's still not close enough. Raking my hands down his back, I clutch him to me, desperate for the feel of his hands on my skin.

"Touch me," I whisper against his lips, arching my back. "Please."

His rough hand trails down my neck to cup my breast, and I gasp at the sensation as his thumb slowly circles my nipple. "Yes," I hiss, arching into his touch even more. His tongue follows the same trail, and I very nearly come undone on the spot. "Oh, God, Brock. I need you, please."

He lifts his eyes to mine, his fingers still kneading my soft flesh.

"Please don't make me beg." I pull my lip between my teeth, rolling my hips up into him. Taking charge, I uncoil my legs from his waist, slide my hands down my body and hook my fingers in the lace of my panties, slipping them down my hips. His eyes watch my every move, his tongue darting out to wet his lips.

"God, you're beautiful." His hands land on mine, taking over until I'm stripped bare before him. "So beautiful," he murmurs again.

Discarding his boxers, he kneels between my thighs, his eyes sweeping up my body to meet mine. What I see in those eyes nearly takes my breath away. He's looking at me like he won the lottery, like I'm the best damn prize there is, and it brings tears to my eyes. No one has ever looked at me that way, not even Bradley, and he was my world once upon a time.

Mistaking my tears for sadness, he whispers, "We don't have to do this if you don't want to." His lips brush across my cheek, wiping my tears away, ever the gentleman. Once again, I'm reminded how lucky I am to have him in my life, that he chose me of all people.

I snake my hands around his neck, pulling him in to me. "How do you make me feel like the most beautiful person in the world with just one look?"

He draws back. "Well that's easy. You are the most beautiful person in the world. How else am I meant to look at you?"

Words escape me as I stare into his eyes so full of sincerity. I can't get enough of this man and the way he makes me feel.

Wrapping my legs around his waist again, I bring him in to me, rocking my hips up to meet his. He slowly sinks deep inside me, and I swear my eyes roll up to the back of my head, it feels that good. Right now, I don't care that he's too good for me. All I can think about is how we're like two pieces of a puzzle finally finding their place together, and damn if it doesn't feel like the only thing that's right in this world.

Chapter twenty-one

Stretching my arms out above me, I grin at the glorious ache of a body finally joining the land of the living again. Our bedroom gymnastics went long into the night, and even though I must be on set in less than an hour, I'm on a high like no other. It would take something catastrophic to bring me down today.

Brock is peacefully sleeping beside me, and like a creeper, I take a moment to watch him. The serenity on his face is quite beautiful, as if he has not a care in the world. It makes me smile to see him so at ease, knowing I had a little something to do with that.

Careful not to disturb him, I slip from the sheets and pad to the bathroom to ready myself for the day. As much as I wish I didn't have to wash his scent from me, I jump in the shower and lather up, giving my body a quick once over. I have no doubt in my mind there will be a repeat performance later, and the thought alone is enough to send shivers of anticipation down my spine. This man is quickly taking over my every thought, and though it should make me nervous to feel so much after such a short time, it doesn't. It just feels right to be in his arms.

Never has heading to a set been so hard before. All I really want to do is curl back up beside him and forget about the world, even for just one day, but something tells me Blake and Bo wouldn't be too impressed with that idea. Right now, they're the only thing between me and the scrap heap of Hollywood has-beens, so it's best I keep them happy.

With keys in hand, I quickly scrawl a note to say he's to make himself at home and I hope to see him waiting for me come evening. Now that I've had my taste of him, the craving is even more intense, and I can't wait for more.

Throwing the pen across the counter, my eyes land on the calendar on the wall. The crosses mark each day passed, and with only a few blank squares left, I'm suddenly hit with a feeling of foreboding.

How can it be that date already?

I've been so preoccupied with my job and Brock that I didn't even realize how close we are to April and the day my world came crashing down around my ears.

Staring at the calendar as if I can somehow turn back time, that familiar unease trickles down my spine, and I wrap my arms around my waist to shield myself from what I know is coming, whether I like it or not.

April 3rd. The day my life changed forever.

Not only does it mark the day I moved here from my hometown of Ashburton to start afresh, it also marks the day one year prior, when I lost my best friend in the whole world; my sister, Sarah.

We were like two peas in a pod, practically joined at the hip. Three years my junior, she had a vibrant way about her, always finding the bright side of life. She had a passion for all things Shakespeare, and her dream was to one day grace the stages of Broadway. She would've knocked their socks off too, that's how good she was.

Every birthday, I would take her to the latest theatre production, and more often than not, I would spend most of my time watching her as the emotions took over and danced across her face. It was better than any other show in town. I guess that's what made her so brilliant to watch; she felt *everything*, perhaps too much. She was one of those people who lit up a room simply by being there. And now every room seems that much duller without her presence.

A tear drips from my chin to the counter, pulling me out of my reverie. I know I need to move past it. I know it's what she would want, but it doesn't stop that soul crushing hurt from weaselling its way into my heart every year. They say it gets easier with time, but it's been four years, and the pain is just as great now as it was then.

I stare at the crumpled note for Brock. My fingers twitch as I fight the urge to throw it in the waste basket, call in sick, and hide away with a bottle of something to ease the pain. Alcohol isn't the answer, I know that, but it's the only thing that dulls the ache in my heart. Not even Brock can do that, not fully.

Squeezing my eyes closed, I rub my temples, trying to find the strength to walk out the door and go to work. Perhaps it's what I need to keep my mind off the impending date.

"Morning."

"Shit!" I swear I jump about three feet in the air, clutching a hand to my chest.

His throaty chuckle rumbles through me as his arms circle my waist from behind. "Sorry. I didn't mean to scare you." He plants a kiss in the crook of my neck, rubbing his stubble against my skin. "It seems to be becoming a habit."

I force a laugh. "I was away with the fairies." Allowing myself to relax into his warmth for a second, I inhale deeply, closing my eyes. "I hope I didn't wake you. I was trying to be quiet."

"You learn to rise with the sun out on the ranch. This is late for me."

I attempt a southern drawl. "You can take the boy outta the country, but you can't take the country outta the boy."

He chuckles again. "Something like that." He spins me to face him, and I hope he can't see the turmoil in my eyes. I want so much to be okay for him. To not have this crippling pain hanging over my shoulder, ready to take me down at a moment's notice.

Plastering a smile to my face, I reach up on tiptoes, grazing my lips across his. "As much as I'd rather be here with you, I have to go."

His eyes search mine, and I curse this pale complexion of mine for giving me away. "Are you okay?" His voice is soft as he strokes a finger down my cheek. "You look like you've been crying."

"Do I? That's weird." I clear my throat, making myself step out of his embrace. Surreptitiously swiping a hand under my eyes, I say, "I'm fine. Just have to get to work or I'll have Blake and Bo knocking down my door." I try to laugh but it sounds forced, even to my ears.

His lips form a tight line, but he doesn't push it. "Will I see you later?"

It's a simple question, but one that proves harder to answer. Do I want to see him later and have him help me forget? Hell yes. Will I be able to come home without a few drinks under my belt? The forecast doesn't look good.

"Emma?"

"Hmm? Oh! Um, yeah. Yes. I mean, if you want to." There. It's done. Decision made. It's out in the universe now, and so it will be. I've got a good thing going with Brock, and I can't let my past ruin it. I won't.

Chapter twenty-two

"Emma! Thank Christ. Come be the voice of reason." Bo's loud voice booms down the corridor as I walk through the door.

Plastering on a smile I'm not really feeling, I hurry towards him. "What seems to be the problem?"

"My brother is losing his mind, that's the problem."

I quirk a brow, looking between the two of them. I can't tell if this is a serious spat or just them being playful. "I'm going to need more information than that."

Bo turns his back on his brother, hooking a thumb over his shoulder. "He's impossible."

Blake winks at me, and I can't help the curl of my lips at these two. One minute they're best friends, the next they're at each other's throats. It's like I've adopted two rather large kids sometimes.

"Bo." I place my hand on his arm. "I still don't understand what's going on, but I'm going to go out on a limb here and say, Blake is right."

Bo throws his hands in the air. "Of course you'd take *his* side." He spins around to an almost bursting-at-the-seams Blake. His shoulders sag and he shakes his head. "Asshole. I thought you were serious!"

"It would put us back weeks. How could you honestly think I'd want to retake the entire movie?" He slaps his hand on Bo's shoulder with a chuckle. "Sometimes you make it too easy, brother."

Watching the two of them sets me at ease. If I can just hold on to this feeling, perhaps I can get through the next week without thinking about Sarah and my guilt too much. It's still too early in the piece to drag Brock down with all my baggage, and even though I know he'd try to make me feel better, I'm not sure I'm ready for that. I'm not ready to see the pity in his eyes, or worse, the blame. It's bad enough when I look in the mirror and see her eyes staring back at me.

"Earth to Emma." Bo clicks a finger in front of my face. "You're needed in makeup so we can get started."

"Right, of course. On it."

I take a seat in the swivel chair and spin to avoid my reflection. I'm on the wire right now, and all it will take is a gentle breeze to tip me over the edge. If I can just get through this and out in front of the camera, I might make it through the day without any more tears.

Yes. Throwing myself into work is the best idea. I don't have time to think about my own things when I'm pretending to be someone else.

***

"Can we do it again? I didn't quite nail it that time. I know I can do better."

Blake pulls me aside. "Is everything okay?"

"Yeah, why wouldn't it be?"

"You seem a little off today, like you're second guessing yourself."

"I just want to make sure I'm giving you my best, that's all."

He purses his lips. "Mmhmm. I don't know what this is, but you need to rein it in. We've already shot this scene five times, and it was fine on the third go around." His eyes search mine. "I'm extremely happy with your work, Emma, and if ever there comes a time when I'm not, I'll let you know, so just relax, okay?"

"Okay, sorry."

"You two lovebirds finished having a heart to heart over there? We've got a movie to shoot." Bo chuckles, muttering, "Get a room" under his breath.

"Is he okay?" I ask.

"Who? Bo?" Blake glances over at his brother who gives us the universal 'hurry it up' signal. "He's fine. Probably eager to go out later and get his end away." He snorts. "He's always got someone lined up."

"Bit of a player, is he?"

"That's an understatement. Trust me, the only reason he hasn't come sniffing around you yet is because he thinks you're with me. As far as he's concerned, anyone else is fair game, and he likes to hunt."

"Come on already. I'd like to get outta here some time this century!" Bo calls out. Blake and I look at each other and laugh.

"Sorry, boss!"

Blake gives my arm a gentle squeeze before walking away. "Places everyone! Javier, you ready?"

"All set... boss." He turns back to his camera, a thin set to his mouth. I don't miss the way Blake falters in his steps at the coldness in Javier's tone. I can understand it must be hard to watch your boyfriend pretend to be in a relationship with someone else, but he doesn't need to be a dick about it. Blake's just doing what he has to to survive in a world where coming out still holds a stigma in some places. He can't help who his father is.

"Scene six, take six." A loud clap of wood sounds through the studio.

"In five, four, three, two, one. Rolling!"

Chapter twenty-three

"Who is this clown?" Bo says as the side door swings open and someone enters the room. "Cut! Everybody take five!" He and Blake both step out from behind the cameras, heading for the door with purpose.

"Excuse me, this is not open to the public. I'm going to have to ask you to leave."

"What? A father can't visit his sons while they work? What's this world coming to?" A well-dressed man with a cigarette hanging from his lips steps out of the darkness.

"Dad?" they both say in unison.

Blake's steps slow, his hands delving into his pockets. "What are you doing here?"

"I was in the neighborhood, thought I'd drop by." He looks around the room as if seeing it for the first time. "You're not going to introduce me to your friends?"

"Ah, yeah, of course." Blake ushers me over. "Emma, this is my father, Marty. Dad, this is Emma Jones."

He takes my hand, bringing it to his lips and maintaining eye contact. There's an air of smugness around him, as though he owns the room and everyone in it. "Emma, it's a pleasure."

"Likewise." I find myself wanting to curtsey under his scrutiny, and a blush colors my cheeks. Pulling my hand back, I turn to Blake with a smile. "You have some extremely talented sons here, Mr Ramirez."

"So I'm told."

My eyes flick back to his with a quirk of my brow. "You haven't seen *All About Frank*?"

"I'll see it when I see it, sweetheart." He waves a hand through the air dismissively. "More pressing business to attend to and what not. I'm sure you can understand." He smirks, puffing a cloud of smoke in my face.

I instantly bristle at the flippant way he's able to blow off the success of his sons. "I think you'll find you're missing out on something monumental. They're the talk of the town."

"Runs in the family." He winks, laughing arrogantly. He's got some nerve. I don't care who he is, it doesn't give him the right to come in here waving his dick around as if he's the only reason they're a hit.

I open my mouth to say so, but Blake steps in. "Bo, why don't you show Dad around the studio, introduce him to the rest of the cast?"

"Sure." He shoves one hand in his pocket, and the other gestures forward. "Right this way, Dad."

Once they're out of earshot, I turn to Blake with a questioning gaze. "He hasn't even seen your movie yet?"

He shifts, watching them walk around the room, and his whole body appears to shrink in on itself. "Some father, eh?"

"He's something alright." I fold my arms across my chest, wondering what it must've been like growing up in the shadows of an overbearing father. Sure, my mother still looks at me with blame, but deep down, I know she still loves me. But this guy? I don't blame Blake for wanting to keep a few secrets.

Bo leads Marty around the camera crew, and I don't miss the way Javier squares himself up to match his stance, almost like he's trying to show his worth to this man who hasn't a clue who he is and how important he is in his son's life.

Blake shuffles from one foot to the other, his teeth nervously chewing on his thumbnail as he watches their interaction.

I take his hand, pulling it away from his lips. "He won't say anything."

"Won't he?" His eyes plead with mine, begging me to give him the answer he needs.

"Of course he won't. He loves you, Blake. It's clear as day."

"But this is what he wants, to tell my family about us."

"Trust me, he's not going to out you in front of a room full of people." His eyes dart back and forth between mine. "He's not your father. As much as he wants the truth out there, he would never do anything to hurt you like that. Have a little faith."

He huffs out a breath, dropping his head into his hands. "You're right. I know he won't. I don't know what's wrong with me."

I pull him into my arms, planting a kiss on his cheek. "There's nothing wrong with you. You just have an ass for a father." His shoulders shake as he chuckles. I lean back with a grin. "There it is. There's that smile."

One eyebrow lifts as he purses his lips. "I could say the same thing about you. I feel like I'm only now getting the real Emma back. The life of the party." He waggles his eyebrows. "Seriously though, is everything okay?"

I shrug. "It's just a rough time of year for me." My voice catches in my throat, and I shake my head, letting him know I don't want to discuss it.

"Hey." His fingertips dig into my hips, stopping me from turning away. "How about we have a drink tonight? I feel like we could both use one."

It's like he can read my mind, only, I'm pretty sure he actually means drink, singular, whereas I can see a whole lot more in my future.

"Come on. You can bring that hot new man of yours so I can meet him."

"How do you know he's hot?"

"Pfft. He managed to snag you, didn't he? One of the hottest names in Hollywood. I'd be surprised if he was any less than an eight."

I can't help but laugh, throwing my arm around his waist as we walk towards the others. "Aww, honey, he's so far off the scale, you wouldn't even believe."

"That hot?" He flaps a hand in front of his face. "Now you definitely need to bring him."

Chapter twenty-four

With a drink under my belt already, and another on the way, I keep an eye on the door, watching for Brock's arrival. I don't think he was too keen to come hang at a bar for the evening, not when we had other things we could be doing, but when I told him Blake would be here and wanted to meet him, he changed his tune.

"I'm nervous. Is that weird?" Blake slides his hands down his thighs. "I feel like I'm meeting your father and asking for permission to date you."

I offer a bemused smile. "Everything'll be fine. He'll just take you out the back and rough you up a bit. No big deal." I lift the glass to my lips, watching his eyes bug out. "Relax! I'm only joking. He'll do it here in front of everyone." I grin.

"It's not funny!"

"It is a little." I hold my finger and thumb up with a tiny gap between them. "Seriously though,

I think it'll be fine. He's the sweetest guy. So kind and generous. He wouldn't hurt a fly." Just thinking about him has me smiling.

"You really like him, don't you?" Blake leans an elbow on the bar. "Maybe even love?"

"I..." Pursing my lips, I search my feelings, wondering if he might be right. "I think maybe I do." The words are out before I even realize what I'm saying, and now that they're out there, I know they're true. I do. I love Brock. I've only known him a few weeks, but in that short amount of time, he's shown me how to live again. I'm not just going through the motions anymore, I'm living, or I was until this morning.

Blake pats a hand on my thigh. "That's great, Emma. I'm happy for you." His gaze flits about the room, never stopping in one place.

"Hey." I reach out, palming his cheek and drawing him to face me. "It doesn't change anything. I'll still be your wingman."

He smiles wistfully. "That can only last so long. Brock won't want to share you forever."

"Yeah, but you don't want this to be a forever thing either, right? You're going to come out eventually, and until then, I'm happy to be by your side."

Taking my hand and placing it across his heart, he smiles, his eyes brimming with unshed tears. "You're a good friend."

"Yeah, I know." I toss my hair over my shoulder. "I'm the shizzle."

Across the room, the door opens, and I'm once again taken by the man stalking towards me. It's like every time is the first time with him. There's something so rugged and manly that always has me catching my breath, and then he smiles, and my legs go to mush.

"Is that him?" Blake asks. By the sound of his voice, I'd be willing to bet Brock is having the same effect on him as he is on me.

"That's him." I sigh like a Disney princess, half expecting birds to flutter in through the windows and fix my hair.

"Emma." Brock places his hand on my lower back, leaning in for a kiss before turning to Blake with an outstretched hand. "And you must be Blake. I've heard so much about you."

Blake raises an eyebrow at me, and I shake my head. I would never betray his trust like that.

"All good, I hope."

"Of course." They shake hands, eyeing each other up. It's insanely hot. I have to force my eyes away before I combust on the spot.

"Can I get you a drink?" Blake waves the bartender over, tapping both our glasses for a refill.

"Soda water is fine." He pulls a chair up to sit between us, his hand resting on my knee.

Poor Blake is sweating it. He keeps rubbing the back of his neck, and his drink is going down much faster than it was before.

I don't think Brock has any idea how intimidating he can be without even trying. He's a man of few words until you get to know him, which can make him seem standoffish, I guess. Couple that with his six-foot stature, and broad shoulders, and you have yourself a winning combo.

"So, um, you're probably wondering why I keep stealing Emma away." Blake laughs nervously, adjusting his shirt collar.

"Not really." Brock meets my eyes, the corner of his mouth pulling up into a half smile. "I trust her." He gives my leg a squeeze.

"All the same, I just want you to know my intentions are purely platonic." He waves his hands in front of him. "I'm not interested in her in that way, whatsoever."

"Hey!" I slap the back of my hand against his chest. I know he's not into women, but does he need to make me sound like I'm the dog's breakfast?

He chuckles. "You know what I mean." He turns to Brock. "I'm... um... she's not my type."

"Okay. I appreciate your wanting to clarify things, but there's really no need. I have no problem with her being friends with another man." He looks at me with sincerity. "Friends are important, and if she ever needs someone to talk to other than me," he turns to Blake, "I'm glad she has you."

His subtle hint isn't lost on me, but for now, I choose to ignore it, focusing on the present. I'm not ready to open that can of worms just yet. No, for now, I'm pushing it down to the depths of hell where it can't hurt me. For now, I'm focusing on what I have, and not what I'm missing.

Chapter twenty-five

I hear her before I see her. The unmistakable click of heels against my tiled foyer echoes down the hall, and I can tell by the cadence, I'm in trouble. My money is on someone snapping a pic of me at the bar last night. One drink turned into several, until Brock was practically dragging me out the door.

I chance a glance at his sleeping form beside me, once again wondering how he puts up with me. I know my drinking isn't his favorite thing in the world, and one of these days, he's going to get sick of me, I just know it. But until then, I'm going to enjoy every last minute I have with him. Especially now that I've realized my true feelings for him. For the first time in a long time, I have something I care too much about to lose.

"What part of lay low and keep away from the booze do you not understand? Oh!" Cybil rounds the corner, stopping short when she sees my sleeping Adonis. I raise a finger to my lips, slipping from the sheets and padding across the room to greet her.

Pulling the door closed behind me, I lead her back towards the kitchen to put on a fresh pot of coffee like a good little hostess. I potter about, trying to ignore the accusatory look in her eyes.

"I'm not going away, you know?" She taps a foot impatiently on the floor until I turn to face her.

"Look, I'm sorry, okay? I'd had a rough day and so had Blake. We needed to debrief, and one drink led to another." I shrug. "What can I say but, I'm sorry?" I fold my arms across my chest, leaning back against the counter.

Cybil sighs. "Contrary to popular belief, I'm not a heartless cow. I do have a soul." Her eyes flick to the calendar. "I know for whatever reason this time of year can be hard on you... but you need to think about your career." She walks over to me, her hand reaching out hesitantly, as if she's afraid I'll disappear if she gets too close. "Maybe you should consider seeing someone. Talk whatever it is out." She purses her lips. "Did you give any consideration to the rehab clinic?" Her words are hushed, and I appreciate that she doesn't want to draw attention to my faults any more than I do.

"The thing Dawn suggested?" I snort, quirking a brow. "You're actually backing her up on that?"

She rolls her eyes. "She does have *some* good ideas. Occasionally." Her face scrunches up as if it hurt to admit it.

The pot on the stove whistles, and I'm thankful for the interruption. Turning my back on her, I grab two cups down. "Coffee?"

"No, thanks. I'm not staying." Her voice softens. "Will you at least think about it?"

Placing my hands on the counter in front of me, I drop my head into my chest. "I appreciate the concern, Cybil, but I don't have a problem." I peer over my shoulder to see her shaking her head. "I don't. I just enjoy a drink or two. What's so wrong with that?"

"It's not the drink or two I'm worried about, it's the other ten that follow."

She doesn't know what she's talking about. I don't *need* to drink. I *want* to drink. There's a difference. I could give up if I wanted to.

I plaster a smile on my face and give her the answer she needs to hear. "Okay, if it means so much to you, I'll think about it, okay?"

"That's all I ask." She places a folded newspaper on the counter before hitching her bag over her shoulder. Tilting her head, she meets my gaze over her glasses. "We don't need any more of these headlines." She holds my gaze for a moment then spins on her heel and strides out.

My eyes skim over the words, "*The Truth Comes Out*", and down to the image of me between Blake and Brock, my arms draped around them both, balancing a glass of vodka in each hand on their shoulders. One eye is half closed, while the other is open, giving me a more than sozzled appearance. Blake is leaning in to me, like he's divulging a secret. His hand resting on my thigh. But Brock looks like he wants to be anywhere but there.

A pang of guilt shoots through me, settling in the pit of my stomach. *How did I not see how uncomfortable he was? How did I not realize?*

I force myself to read the blurb beneath and see what 'truth' they think has come out. My eyes gloss over as I read how I seduced Blake and that's how I got the lead role of Taylor in his up and coming production. They've labeled me a tramp, saying I'm anyone's after a few drinks. There's another picture underneath it of Brock escorting me out at the end of the night. He has his arms wrapped firmly around me, but my head is on a weird angle and it looks as though I can barely walk.

Jesus.

I drop my head into my hands with a groan.

"I'm not surprised." Brock walks towards me, and I quickly crumple the paper and throw it in the trash where he can't see it. He looks at the waste basket then back at me but doesn't say a word. Instead, he grabs the other coffee cup and pours himself a drink.

"I guess I got a little drunk last night?"

He quirks a brow. "A little?" Shaking his head, he laughs though I can tell he thinks it's anything but funny. "That's an understatement."

I offer a weak smile. "Did you have a good time though? Blake's nice, right?" I keep seeing the look on his face in that picture. The look that screamed, get me out of here.

"Yeah, he's a stand up guy." Something in his tone tells me otherwise.

I swallow the lump in my throat. "Are you mad at me?"

He sighs, raking a hand through his hair. "No. I'm not mad at you." He reaches for my hand, pulling me over to him. "I like Blake, and he seems rather taken with you too. I just hope he's not... encouraging things."

I lean back, a frown settling on my face. "Encouraging things? You mean like drinking?" *What is it with everyone today?*

"I..." He shakes his head. "Never mind. You have a few days off, right? Maybe I could take you out to the ranch? Show you around?"

If it means he'll stop looking at me like someone who needs fixing, then I'm all for it. "Sure, sounds fun."

"Great. You're going to love it. Wide open spaces, fresh country air. It'll be good for you. For us." He kisses my forehead. "I'll just grab a shower then we can go."

"Mmhmm." I watch him walk away, knowing it's only a matter of time before he does that for good.

Chapter twenty-six

I was reluctant to hand the keys to Betsy over, but it was either that or ride in his hulking big F150, which is virtually impossible for my not-so-long legs to climb up into. And now that Brock is sitting behind the bright pink steering wheel with fluffy dice dangling in front of him, I'm quite pleased with my decision. There's nothing sexier than a manly man driving his girlfriend's pink convertible.

If I'm honest, it's quite nice sitting back and letting him take the wheel. I can actually enjoy the scenery as it passes us by. I feel like a kid on my first proper road trip.

The entire three years I've been out here in Hollywood, I've not ventured out of LA. It's not that I didn't want to—I've always thought it'd be cool to do a cross-country drive through all the states—but for the first wee while I could barely string enough money together to pay for rent and food, and then when the money started rolling in,

I was just too busy. There was always something else I needed to do, or somewhere I needed to be. I guess life just got in the way for a bit.

This trip out to see the ranch where Brock grew up is just what I need to keep my mind off things. From the very first moment I laid eyes on him, I could picture him working the land or riding bare back on a horse, so to be able to experience it first-hand is something I'm really looking forward to.

The closer we get, the more relaxed he seems to get too. The lines creasing his forehead earlier have vanished, and he has a contented smile upon his face. I vow to make sure it stays that way. As of right now, I'm putting the article behind me, ignoring the date, and enjoying our time away together.

Glancing briefly at me, he takes my hand and brings it to his lips. "You doing okay?"

"Mmhmm." I stretch my free arm out in front of me. "Enjoying the scenery, actually."

"Where have you been other than LA? Grand Canyon? Vegas?"

I shake my head. "Nope and nope. I've been a bit of a home body, I'm afraid."

"You haven't been anywhere else? Anywhere at all?"

"Nope." I shrug. "I always thought it'd be cool to do the *Thelma and Louise* cross-country drive thing, but without my sister, it just doesn't feel right. She was the one who really wanted to live here, not me. I'm kinda doing it for her, if that makes sense."

Brock kisses my hand again, placing it on his lap with a contented smile. "Thank you."

"For what?"

"You've never spoken about her before. In fact, that's the first glimpse I've had into your life before moving here." He chuckles. "I was beginning to think you'd just appeared out of thin air."

"Oh." I don't know what else to say. I hadn't meant to open up about it, and I've no intention of continuing that conversation either.

Sensing my unease, Brock squeezes my hand. "It's okay. We can talk about something else if you want to."

I smile, grateful he understands. "Thanks." I turn to look back out the window. "So, where exactly are we going?"

"Just on the outskirts of Phoenix, Arizona. Far enough away from the city to appreciate the night sky." He grins, those dimples of his peeking out. "I used to lie on the back of Dad's pick-up truck at the end of the day and just watch. It's so clear up there, the stars almost look like crystals. We might even see a shooting star if we're lucky."

"Sounds beautiful."

He tucks a hair behind my ear, his palm cupping my cheek. "Not nearly as beautiful as you." My heart melts just a little bit more, and I nuzzle into his hand. Lines like that always sounded so cheesy in the movies, but when it comes from Brock, it's different. It sounds real, like maybe it might be true. And once again, I find myself wondering how I got to be so lucky.

***

We pull up a long dirt track lined with lush green trees. Cattle graze in fields either side of us. Some lift their heads to watch us pass them by, while others take no notice of the bright pink car cruising along the path.

The drive curves to the left, and the house in front is everything I imagined it would be. Standing two stories high, the deep brown of the wood looks as though it grew up from the earth it stands on. Green shutters line the windows, and a large covered veranda wraps around the entire house. It's both extravagant and homely all in one. I can almost picture a young Brock racing around the pillars lining the veranda.

"Wow," I breathe, my jaw dropping in a very unladylike fashion. "This place is magnificent."

That smile I've come to crave stretches across his face as he pulls the car around to park. "Wait till you see inside."

Leaving our bags in the car, he takes my hand and leads me up the step to the front door. It has one of those brass knockers in the center; two horses heads, back to back, with a horseshoe for the knocker. The handle itself is ornate, with vines wrapping down its length.

Brock unlocks the door and pulls me through to a large entryway. A stone fire sits directly in front of us, its flames already warming the room.

To the left is an archway through to the kitchen, and to the right is the living area.

"Come on, I'll show you around." He squeezes my hand, leading me through the house. The kitchen has an old ceramic stove with an iron kettle on top, and pots and pans hang above from a rack. The island bench has a granite top that glistens under the warm lights. It looks like something out of a Home and Garden magazine, and I can't quite believe it's real.

We move through to the dining area which sits behind the fire of the entryway. A large oak table sits pride of place, its edges rough and gnarly. Long bench seats line each side.

I can tell he's put a lot of himself into the place, while also keeping his parents' memories alive. Throughout the house are photos of the family, and it's obvious the love that filled this home once upon a time. My heart fills with sadness to think he lost that so early on in life, and at the same time, pride at how he can still show such love and warmth after being dealt that blow.

He pulls me up the staircase, my fingers trailing along the wall as I take in more images of his childhood. Those gorgeous dimples of his were prevalent even then.

My eyes land on a snapshot of Brock and his mom, their heads thrown back in laughter.

"She had the best sense of humor." He smiles, his eyes bright. "She was always laughing."

"Looks like she was a lot of fun."

"She really was." He leans in to kiss behind my ear. "You remind me of her sometimes."

"I do?" Warmth fills my chest and spreads through my body at the compliment.

"You have that same light in your eyes, and you're not afraid to be yourself." He brushes a finger down the side of my face, tilting my chin. His lips press lightly to mine. "Come on." He nods his head towards the landing. "You're going to love this."

We reach the top and he leads me past closed doors. "These are all spare bedrooms," he explains as we pass. "But this is what I wanted to show you." He stands to the side, sweeping a hand through a doorway.

If my jaw dropped at the exterior of the house, it's well and truly hit the floor now. The whole room is full of flickering candles, and the scent of jasmine fills the air. A beautiful claw foot tub sits under a large bay window overlooking the ranch.

"How did you...?" I trail my fingers through the warm water.

He tucks his hands in his pockets, rocking back on his heels. "I had Henry draw it ready for our arrival."

"And you say I'm full of surprises." I grin up at him, wrapping my hands around his neck. "This is perfect." I inhale deeply. "You're perfect."

He puffs his chest out, a grin settling on his face, and it's the most adorable thing I've ever seen.

"Are you going to join me?" I step back towards the bath, holding his gaze as I slowly begin to undress.

His Adam's apple bobs as he swallows, a heat filling his eyes as he unbuttons his shirt.

I shrug my blouse from my arms, letting it drop to the floor around my feet. Reaching my arms behind me, I unclasp my bra, then circle it through the air before letting it fling over to land at his feet, because I'm awkwardly sexy like that.

His eyes drop to the piece of fabric then back up to me with a smirk. "I don't think it's my size."

"Aww, go on. You'd make a beautiful woman." I waggle my eyebrows with a giggle.

He unbuckles his pants, pushing them to the floor. "Is that so?"

Now it's my turn to swallow, my teeth clamping on to my bottom lip as I take him in. I don't think I'll ever get sick of seeing him in all his naked glory. The man looks as though he's carved from stone, the perfect specimen of man. It's almost unfair.

With a crook of my finger, I beckon him to me. He wastes no time, his feet eating up the tiles in mere seconds until his chest is pressed against mine. His firm, muscular chest.

God, he's beautiful, and he's *mine*.

We stand there, our bodies panting with need as our eyes devour each other.

Taking his hand, I step back, tentatively dipping a toe into the warm water of the bath. It's the perfect temperature, and the scent wafting up as the water ripples is divine.

The fact that he had this all planned out astounds me. He's so thoughtful and perceptive.

It's like he knows what I need before I do sometimes. "Remind me again how you haven't been snatched up already?" I tug on his hand, pulling him into the water with me.

"I guess I was just waiting for the right one." He shrugs, settling in behind me, and I swear, a tear comes to my eye. How can he be so sure about me when *I'm* not even that sure about me? Sometimes the guilt I hold over Sarah weighs me down so much I can barely stand to be around myself, and here he is, saying I'm the one he was waiting for, like I'm so much more than I am.

I'm about to say as much when he picks up the soap and distracts me with those magic fingers of his. My head rolls forward, enjoying the sensual way he kneads my body. I hadn't noticed quite how tense I was until this very moment, and now, under the skilful work of his fingers, I can feel it all drain away as if it wasn't there in the first place.

"God, that feels good." I peek over my shoulder at him. "I think you missed your calling."

One side of his mouth turns up in a lopsided grin, and I can't believe it's even possible, but it's somehow more endearing than the dimples I've come to love so much.

"Can you imagine people paying for these rough hands on their bodies?" He shakes his head with a chuckle. "I don't think so."

"Oh, I think so. You're underestimating the randiness of these Hollywood socialites. They'd practically throw themselves at you. I mean, look at you." I angle my body towards him, waving a hand through the air in front of him. "You're like every girl's wet dream personified." I tap a finger to my chin. "Hmm, there could be something in this. Maybe I should start pimping you out."

He throws his head back, laughing, and water spills over the sides of the tub. "I'm sorry to burst your bubble, but I'm a one-woman man. These hands are for your pleasure alone." As he says it, he brings his hands up to rub my neck, and I groan, sinking further into the water.

"You know what? I like the sound of that. Those hands are *my* pleasure tools. I don't think I could share you with anyone else, even if they *were* paying the big bucks."

"I'm glad you feel that way." He leans down, brushing his lips against the shell of my ear as his hands trail down to wrap around my waist. "I don't like to share either." I know he's meaning Blake, but I don't know what to tell him without breaking that confidence.

His teeth drag along my neck then he peppers kisses over the same trail, making it hard for me to think straight. I tilt my head further, giving in to the sensation. Tingles run up and down my spine with every touch until I'm quivering with need, but I know he's waiting for that confirmation. That nod to say, I'm all his and no one else's.

"Please, Brock," I whisper, writhing against him. "Please. I'm yours."

He pauses, his breath coming out in short pants. "Are you?"

I turn to face him, coming up onto my knees and wrapping my arms around his neck. "I'm only yours, I swear."

His grin stretches across his face as his arms wrap firmly around me, crushing me to his chest. "Well that's good enough for me."

Chapter twenty-seven

"You've really never been on a horse before?" He stands there with his hands on his hips and a cocky smirk on his face. "What kind of an upbringing did you have over there?" If it wasn't such a sexy look on him, I think I'd almost feel offended.

Folding my arms across my chest, I jut my chin. "The good kind. Playing tag with the other kids on our street, pretending we could fly by jumping off the back of Dad's old HQ Holden." I hold my arms out wide and close my eyes with my head tipped back. "We really did think we could fly back then," I say wistfully before turning back to him. "We were city slickers through and through. I don't even remember seeing a real live horse until I was a teenager – at least, not one I could get up close enough to pat."

He shakes his head. "You haven't lived until you've ridden a horse." He runs his hand down the neck of a chestnut mare. "There's nothing comes close to it."

"Well, I'll have to take your word for it, I guess."

He looks at me with one eyebrow raised. "No, you won't."

"Ah, yeah, I will." I widen my stance, placing my hands on my hips defiantly. If he thinks for a second that I'm going to get on that thing, he's got another think coming.

"Emma?"

"Yes?"

"Are you... scared of horses?" His tone is soft, but he's looking at me as if I'm insane. Grabbing the rein, he slowly leads the mare towards me, but I jump back, my arms held out in front of me.

"What are you doing?" My eyes flick between the horse and Brock, my heart pounding in my chest.

He stops, whispering something to the horse. "I was just going to bring her a little closer, so you could have a pat. She's very docile; she wouldn't hurt a fly."

"But... she's so... big."

He chuckles, smoothing a hand down her mane. "I suppose she might seem that way if you haven't been around them much. She's actually one of our smaller horses here."

I swallow. "There are bigger ones?"

"Sure." He turns, pointing across the field. "My horse, Maddox, is the black one. He's at least another hand taller." Turning back to the horse in front of him, he says, "This one was my mother's."

There's a reverent look in his eye, and it breaks me. It obviously means a lot to him, and I'll be damned if I'm going to ruin something he treasured with his mother.

Edging closer, I ask, "What's her name?"

"Gale."

"Gale? I thought it'd be something like Beauty or Honey."

"Nah, she's Gale because she runs like the wind." He smirks. "Mom always thought she was a bit of a comedian."

I can't help but grin. "You must've had a lot of fun together."

"We did. She would've loved you."

I duck my head, feeling a blush color my cheeks. "I'm sure I would've loved her too." Taking another tentative step forward, I reach a hand out in front of me, stretching as far as I can.

"She won't bite." He takes hold of my hand. "May I?"

Sinking my teeth into my bottom lip, I nod. "Okay," I whisper.

He brings my hand up to rub down Gale's nose. She flicks her head up and down, huffing out a breath, but she stays there, letting me touch her.

"She's so soft." I step in a little closer still, bringing my other hand up slowly to rub between her ears. "Hi, Gale." She snorts, bobbing her head again.

"Not so scary now?"

"I suppose not." I pin him with my stare. "I'm still not getting on her though."

***

"Oh my god!" I throw my head back in a giggle. "I'm doing it! I'm actually doing it!"

Brock's husky laugh rumbles through the air. "Yes, you are."

"I can't believe I've never done this before. It's so exhilarating!" I'm babbling. I know I am, because that's what I do when I'm nervous, and I am *really* nervous. Don't get me wrong, horses are beautiful, majestic creatures, but I have always preferred to admire them from afar. Like way far afar. And now look at me, perched atop Gale's back, my hands white-knuckling the reins as if my life depended on it, because it does. I don't care that she's not a big horse, she's huge to me, and the ground seems a long way from where I'm sitting. But it's oh so worth the fear to see the world from up here.

Maddox huffs, stamping a foot into the dirt. He's a monster of a horse, but Brock looks right at home on his back. I can see now why he wants to be back here. This place is a part of him. It's who he is. It's where he's meant to be, not in the bright lights of Hollywood.

"This place suits you."

I'm taken aback. "Me? How do you figure that?"

He shrugs. "You're more relaxed here, not weighed down by your thoughts." He taps a finger to the side of his head.

In a way, I suppose he's right. I haven't felt the need for a drink since we left LA, and everything else has just been pushed to the back of my mind. I've been enjoying the moments, savoring our time away. Something about this place puts me at ease, and Brock might have a little something to do with it too.

"I feel..." I take a deep breath, closing my eyes briefly. "Free, I guess." I chance a glimpse at him. "Is that weird?"

"Why would it be weird?"

I shrug. "I don't know. Because I'm living the life that others only dream about. I get to pretend I'm someone else every day and get paid to do it. I drive a car like Miss Penelope, and my boyfriend is a hot cowboy. What have I got to complain about?"

Brock chuckles, bringing Maddox to a stop. "Hot cowboy, eh?"

I roll my eyes. Of course that's what he got out of it. "He's all right, I guess." I poke my tongue out teasingly.

There's a hint of a smile on his face, but it's soon lost, his brow furrowing. "You know it's okay if you're not happy doing what you do, right?"

"What's not to be happy about?" There it is. That guilt rearing its ugly head again, and just when I was starting to relax.

"You said yourself, this isn't where you wanted to be. You're doing this for your sister." He pauses, rubbing a hand across his stubbled jaw. "But what is it that *you* want?"

I open my mouth to speak but stop. What *is* it that I want? I've never really thought about it before, and no one's ever stopped to ask me either. Why hasn't anyone asked me that? Why haven't *I* asked me that?

Tears spring to my eyes, and I quickly swipe a hand across my face before they have the chance to fall.

"I don't know what I want," I whisper.

What I want is to run away from this conversation.

I twist in my seat, swinging one leg over to join the other, as I search for a place to get down.

"Whoa, what are you doing?" Brock is up and out of his saddle faster than I can string two thoughts together. His hands steady me as I slide down Gale's side. "What's going on?"

"I just... I need to..." My lungs gasp for air as I push out of his arms. Doubling over, I grasp my knees and suck in large gulps of air.

Brock drops to his knees, one hand stroking my hair away from my face. "Baby, what's wrong? What is it?"

"I don't know," I cry, swiping angry tears from my face before meeting his gaze. "I don't know."

Chapter twenty-eight

"Here, drink this." A steaming cup of tea is thrust before me as Brock takes a seat across the table from me. "My mother always said a cup of tea can do wonders for the soul. I don't know what that was out there, but I think you could use it right now." His brow is furrowed, and he's watching me like he thinks I'm a flight risk.

"I'm sorry. I don't know what that was either." I shrug, blowing the steam from the cup. "I guess I panicked a little."

"But why? What's so wrong with asking you what you want?" He reaches across, his hand feathering over mine until I turn my palm up to meet his. "Help me understand."

Glancing out the window, I pull my lip between my teeth. "The past three years, I've lived my life for her." Tears fill my eyes again, and I curse myself for giving in so easily. It's not his burden to bear.

"But why? Why live for her when you have your own life to live?"

I pull my hand away, leaning back in the chair with a shake of my head. "You wouldn't understand."

Mimicking my stance, he leans back too, huffing out a breath. "I can't if you won't let me in."

My eyes flick up to his. "That's not fair," I whisper. "You said you wouldn't push, so please, just let it go."

His fingers tap against the table and he purses his lips before leaning forward. "Okay."

"Okay?"

"If that's what you want, I won't push. Just know that I'm here whenever you're ready to talk about it."

Fresh tears sting my eyes, and this time, I let them fall. Pushing up from the table, I walk around to him and slide one leg across until I'm straddling him. His arms wrap around my waist and his lips press to my forehead. "Why are you so good to me?"

He tilts my chin up, pressing his lips to mine. "Because that's what you deserve." I try to shake my head, but he holds me firm. "You do. You deserve nothing but the best, and I intend on showing you that until you believe it yourself. And then I'm going to show you some more."

If he didn't already have my heart, he certainly does now. I only hope that when I do finally share my story with him, he'll still feel the same way.

***

True to his word, Brock doesn't push me to talk, and I feel the pressure slowly ebb away as we stroll hand in hand around the ranch. He points out sentimental spots, and I can tell there was a lot of love here. From the tree with his parents' names carved into it, to the creek where he would fish with his father, the whole place is filled with memories.

"I wish we didn't have to go back tomorrow." I sigh as we take a seat on the veranda. The sun begins its slow descent, and we watch in silence as the light fades and the stars come out to play.

It's so peaceful and quiet but for the rustling of grass and the pitter patter of hooves.

"That's how I feel every time I come home. It gets harder and harder to tear myself away and head back to the big smoke." He squeezes my hand. "Of course, I never had you to go back to then."

"Maybe we could come back when shooting is finished? Stay a while?"

"I'd like that." He brings my hand up to his lips with a smirk. "I'll make a cowgirl of you yet."

I snort. "I can see it now. I'll dress in plaid shirts tied at the front with my hair pulled up in pigtails like Ellie-May Clampett."

Brock whistles low. "Now that's a sight I'd like to see." Pulling his hat from his head, he fans it in front of him.

I lean back with a quirk of the brow. "Oh I see, a bit of an Ellie-May fan, are we?" He blushes, and I can't help myself, I put on a hillbilly accent. "Well, hey there little critter." I waggle my eyebrows, climbing onto his lap. "You wanna wrestle?"

His hands go straight to my hips and slide down to my ass. In one fluid motion, he stands, wrapping my legs around his waist. "I sure do."

Giggling, I take his hat and put it on my head, pointing towards the door. "Then giddyup, cowboy!"

Chapter twenty-nine

The drive home is bittersweet. Our mini vacation has brought us closer, but also brought to light a few home truths. It's only a matter of time before he's going to want to leave and head back home for good, and I won't be the one to stand in his way. Not when he so obviously belongs there.

But could I uproot myself and follow him if he asked me to? Part of me is screaming yes, while the other part is leery. This is all I've known for the past three years. I've lived and breathed for Sarah, and up until recently, that's been enough for me. I've never wanted to do anything else, because, well, I never really had any other options as far as I was concerned. Sarah didn't get to live out her dreams because of me, so I'm doing it for her. But, is it so wrong to want a little something for myself? To want something to call my own?

If I close my eyes, I can see a future out there on the ranch. Just me and Brock, tending the land together, making a life, a family. I even think she would be happy that I'm happy, but still, in the back of my mind, there's that nagging feeling. That guilt.

Slogging it out in Hollywood is both a reward and a punishment. I get to hob-nob with some of the world's most glamorous people, I have more money than I've ever had in my life, and I get to go to work each day and play pretend. But I also have access to anything I want, and it's so hard to say no when it's all so tempting. Even now, I can feel the pull of alcohol, and we're not even in the city limits. It's surreal, to say the least.

Maybe ranch life is what I need. Far away from the temptations that pull me down into a spiral of guilt and shame.

I shake my head, chuckling softly to myself. I'm getting ahead of myself here. We haven't even said the L word, and I'm over here picturing us riding off into the sunset to live happily ever after.

It's a nice dream though. One I can hold onto and cherish. One I can perhaps revisit after this shoot is done and I have no ties here.

"Everything okay?" Brock places his hand on my thigh. "You look like you're deep in thought."

"Oh." I wave a hand through the air, letting it fall on top of his. "Just missing the country life already." I smile. "Thank you, by the way. You were right, it was just what I needed."

"No need to thank me. I see how hard you work, and I think sometimes you forget to take care of yourself." He turns to me with a grin. "But you don't have to worry about that anymore, because that's why I'm here."

"That's sweet of you, and I appreciate it. I feel rejuvenated. Must be all the country air out there."

"Sure is. Country air can cure all that ails you, if you let it." He doesn't elaborate, but he doesn't have to. I know he's still hoping I'll talk to him about Sarah, but the thought of telling him scares me almost as much as the knowledge she's not coming back. Things are so good between us right now, and I couldn't bear it if he were to look at me with that same blame in his eyes as my mother does, as I do. I know it's selfish, but I just want to keep him that little bit longer before I shatter our little bubble. I can't bear the thought of losing him too, and when he finds out the truth, that's exactly what will happen.

***

It's 3AM and I'm due on set in two hours. Brock sleeps peacefully beside me, unaffected by my tossing and turning through the night. All I've been able to think about since we walked through the door last night was the alcohol stashed in my cupboard, and the emergency bottle hidden in the garage.

I had no need for it out on the ranch, but now that we're back, the temptation is like nothing else. My tongue is thick, my throat parched. I would give anything for a taste, but something holds me back. Those little devils sit on my shoulder; one coaxes while the other admonishes. I'm torn between tipping the lot down the drain so it's no longer a temptation or downing a bottle to ease the craving. I know which one I should do, but it's getting my body to cooperate that's the problem.

Every time I make my mind up, I'm overcome with a panic that renders me immobile. I can't move for fear of having nothing left for those times of need. It's crazy that a bottle of booze can have this effect on me, but it does. It has a hold on me so tight that I'm afraid of what will happen if I let go.

Just a little taste, then you'll be fine.

I close my eyes to shut it out, but even in the darkness, the voice still taunts me, reminding me of the blissful numbing that comes from my liquid friend.

Maybe just a mouthful...

Pushing the sheets back, I slip from bed on soundless feet. I move swiftly down the hallway towards the kitchen, the urgency of the voice carrying me faster than necessary.

Almost breathless, I eye the cupboard that holds my stash. It's not too late to do the right thing and tip it out.

My fingers drum lightly on the counter as I mull it over, but it's pointless. I know it's inevitable.

I reach out, my fingers grazing the handle before taking hold and wrenching it towards me.

The bottle is in my hands before I can even blink, and when I open the lid, I inhale the fumes right down to my lungs. Closing my eyes, I tip it back, pouring a steady stream into my mouth until I've had my fill. I swipe a hand across my mouth to catch any droplets, then quickly place it back where I got it from.

I tiptoe back to the bedroom, slip under the sheets, and lie there with a new layer of guilt washing over me.

Chapter thirty

"Emma, hi. How are you?" With his hand to my lower back, Blake leads me off to the side. He takes both my hands, staring into my eyes with worry. Either he's breaking up with me, or he's worried about the article.

"It's okay, Blake. I'm fine. I'm kinda used to the stories by now." I wave a hand through the air.

"It's not fine. They made you out to be some sort of bed-hopping floosy. I want you to know we've got our PR people on it. We don't take too kindly to things like that."

"Well, thank you. I was shocked when I read it, but I kinda put it behind me. Let them talk if they want."

He takes hold of my elbow, leaning in close. "What about Brock? Did he see it?"

A blush colors my cheeks as I duck my head. "I might've thrown it in the trash before he got a chance."

"Good. But, Emma? I'll put him straight if I have to. You've helped me out to no end, but I won't have this ruin your reputation."

My eyes widen. "I would *never* expect you to do that for me. I was the one who came up with the idea in the first place by making it appear that way to Bo." I fling my arms around him, holding tight. "When you come out, it's going to be because you're ready and you want to, not because you think you need to save me, okay?" I pull back, looking him square in the eye. "Promise me."

He shakes his head, sighing. "You're not going to let this go, are you?"

I shake my head. "Nope." Crossing my arms across my chest, I quirk a brow, tapping one foot on the ground impatiently. "I'm waiting."

He chuckles, looping his arm around my shoulder. "Okay, I promise."

"Say the words."

"I promise I won't come out unless you say I can."

I slap the back of my hand across his chest. "That's not what I meant."

"All right." He holds up three fingers. "I promise I won't come out until I'm ready to, and not a moment sooner. Happy?"

"Very."

"Christ, you're a handful. I don't envy Brock. He must have the patience of a saint." He barks out a deep, throaty laugh.

"I don't know what you're talking about. I'm a delight to be around." I flash him a grin. "But enough about me. What's on the agenda for today."

He stops walking, taking hold of my shoulders. "First, we need to get you in to makeup and deal to those bags under your eyes." He purses his lips, a hint of laughter in his eyes. "I know we told you to enjoy your break, but we actually wanted you to return rested, not looking like you've been up all night, making whoopee."

"Did you actually just use the term, 'making whoopee'? Do people even say that anymore?"

"Of course they do. I just said it, didn't I?" He winks. "If it was good enough for the fabulous Ella Fitzgerald, it's good enough for me."

"I'm not gonna argue with that, but I will say, if Javier lets you call it that, he's definitely a keeper. You need to put a ring on it, pronto." I giggle, waggling my fingers at him.

"Hmm, we'll see."

"Uh-oh. Trouble in paradise?"

His eyes flick over to Javier briefly. "Nothing I can't handle." Then just like that, he's back to business. He turns me towards the dressing rooms. "Go and get your drunk face on. We've got work to do."

You're the boss...

***

Yeah, I know he didn't mean it in the literal sense, but it didn't stop me from taking a quick swig in the bathroom before taking my place in front of the mirrors. He may have joked about my bags, but I think they add depth to our leading lady. After all, she's a drunk, and I'm well on my way.

I didn't manage to keep that promise to myself; that I'd only need a taste. That taste added fuel to the flame, and even though I'd been lying in bed, laden with guilt, it didn't stop me from pouring myself a hip flask for the road, after inhaling another large mouthful, of course.

So, now that my drunk face is well and truly on, I make my way out to the set, plonking myself down on the couch. "Ready when you are, big guy." I salute no one in particular, then stretch my arm along the back of the couch.

Blake frowns as he makes his way to his chair, and when he tips his head towards me, I nod.

"Just getting into character."

He chuckles, shaking his head. He doesn't need to know exactly *how* into character I am right now. Lord knows I don't need yet another lecture on my alcohol consumption. I've got it under control.

"Places, everyone!" Bo stalks across the room, nodding to the girl holding the clapper board. She quickly scurries in front of Javier, holding it up.

"Scene four, take one!" The clap rings out through the room and she ducks away.

"In five, four, three..." Two and one are mouthed and then he points to me. Taking a deep breath, I stumble across the room much like I had in the audition for this very same scene.

"Hey, baaaaby."

"You're drunk."

"Pssh." I wave a hand through the air dismissively. "Nooooo." I walk towards him, overexaggerating my wobbly legs before falling into his arms with a giggle. "Okay, maybe juss a lil bit." I hold my finger and thumb up.

"Jesus, Taylor, how'd you get home? Please tell me you didn't drive." He props me up, then rakes a hand through his hair.

"Ummm." Sucking my lips in, I pull my finger and thumb across my mouth like a zip. "Wooden you like ta know."

He takes hold of my arms, shaking me. "You realize you could've killed someone, or worse, yourself! What about the kids?" He's looking at me with such anger, that I almost forget we're only acting. Something about this conversation feels too close to home.

Tears spring to my eyes as I whisper, "Don't be like that." I tilt my head up to meet his gaze, swallowing thickly. "I'm fine."

"No, you're not." He shrugs away from me, stalking across the room. "I can't do this anymore."

Focus, Emma. It's not Brock saying this.

"You can't go," I whisper. "Please, don't leave me."

"Cut!"

I blink, looking around the room.

"Nice ad-libbing," Simon says, patting my arm. "I really felt it in here." He taps his chest.

I nod, offering a small smile before peeking over at Blake. He gives me a thumbs up, and I breathe a sigh of relief. They may not have been able to see what that was, but I can still feel it lingering. That feeling that I'm acting out a scene from my own future.

Chapter thirty-one

"Again?" Brock sighs, rubbing his temples. "I know it's a work thing, but this is the third night this week."

I look away, unable to maintain eye contact while I blatantly lie to his face. It's actually only the first time this week. The other two times were just me going to a bar after work and pretending I was with Blake. A dumb move, I know, but it was easier than having him question why I've been drinking again. At least under the guise of a work do, he knows it's expected.

"I know. I'm sorry." I pull at the collar of my blouse, suddenly feeling restricted. "It's the last time, I promise."

"Okay. You've got to do what you've got to do, I guess." He rakes a hand through his hair. "Can you at least have dinner with me first?"

I glance over to the kitchen to see two plates set out with candles between them. Tears prick my eyes, but I bite my lip to stop them from falling and nod instead. "Mmhmm. Sure." Forcing a smile to my face, I wrap my arms around his neck. "Thank you."

His lips brush against mine, and I'm thankful I had the forethought to pop a mint before coming through the door.

"You're too good to me." I press my lips to the base of his neck, inhaling his masculine scent. "I don't deserve you."

He tilts my head up to meet his with a finger under my chin. "You deserve everything I have to offer and more." His voice is husky, and a part of me regrets taking Blake up on his offer to go out tonight.

"Maybe I could call him and cancel. A night in would be nice." Even as I say it, I know I won't. Not tonight.

"It would be, but I know you couldn't do that to Blake." He presses a kiss to the tip of my nose. "You're too good to let anyone down."

I turn my eyes away to the dinner laid out on the bench. I can't handle the way he stares at me like he can see into my soul. It scares me to think what he'll see if he stares too hard.

"This looks nice," I say, pulling away from his arms and pointing at the counter. "Any particular occasion?"

"You tell me." He nods at the calendar on the wall, and the red circle drawn around April 3rd. "Is it your birthday?"

I stare at the red ink wrapping around the date like a noose. I don't even know why I did it, to be honest. It's not like I could ever forget that date, it's engraved on my heart and in my soul.

"Emma?"

"Uh, no. Not my birthday." I shake my head, forcing myself to look away. "My birthday is in June."

"Oh, okay." His eyes flick to the calendar with a frown, but he doesn't say anything. Moving around to the oven, he pulls out a cupcake with a candle in it. "I guess I won't be needing this then." He chuckles. "I know it's corny, but I thought it would be a nice surprise."

I smile, though tears fill my eyes. "Thank you," I whisper, turning my eyes upward to stop the tears from falling.

"Emma? What is it?" He points at the calendar again. "What does this mean?" He stalks towards me, his arms bracing against my shoulders. "Talk to me."

I shake my head as a sob falls from my lips. "I can't do this right now." I turn on my heels and run.

Chapter thirty-two

With my head in my hands, I take deep gulping breaths to calm myself. I hate that I just ran out on him like that, but I couldn't take it anymore. I couldn't stand there and pretend that I am who he thinks I am.

Ironic, isn't it? I pretend for a living, but pretending in front of the man I love is a step too far. I don't know how much longer I can keep it up, and I don't know how much longer he'll let me either. The sands of time are slipping through my fingers and I can't get them to stop and go back, no matter how much I want them to.

A knock at the window has me flinging back in my seat, a hand flying to my chest.

"You okay in there?" Blake's worried frown peers through the glass.

I nod, holding up my purse. "Just touching up my makeup. Be out soon." Clearing my throat, I adjust the rear-view mirror so I can see myself, and I gasp at the unruly look upon my face. I'm a mess. Smears of mascara coat my cheeks, and my eyes are red-rimmed. My hair is still in the loose topknot I'd worn at work, more than a few tendrils floating around my face and clinging to my wet cheeks.

With a tissue, I dab at my face until the black is gone, and quickly reapply my foundation and lipstick. There's still traces of mascara on my lashes, and I leave it that way, not wanting to hold Blake up any longer than necessary.

I unlock the door and push it open. Blake offers his hand and I take it with a smile. *I can do this.*

"Are you sure you're okay?" His stare is piercing.

"Right as rain," I say with forced enthusiasm. "Shall we?" I link my arm through his. "You know, for someone who doesn't like the guy, you sure like to be around him a lot."

"It's all about appearances." He pats my hand. "The academy loves him, and as much as I don't like him, I can't fault his knowledge of the ins and outs of everything that goes on around here. He's someone who can make or break you, so it pays to have him on your side."

We enter the foyer, shrugging off our coats and leaving them with the attendee. I swipe a glass of champagne off a passing tray and tip it back. I can tell I'm going to need more of these to get through this evening.

"Blake, Emma." Tony swans in, waving a cigar through the air. "So glad you could make it." He takes my hand and brings it to his lips, letting them linger longer than socially appropriate. Blake clears his throat, and Tony pulls back with a chuckle. "Possessive, isn't he?" His meaty hand falls to his middle as he laughs.

Playing the part, I laugh along with him, but my arm snakes around Blake, pulling him close to me. There's something about Tony that rubs me the wrong way, and it's not just the misogynistic attitude he has towards me.

A pretty little blonde, teetering on ridiculous heels approaches, draping herself across him. "Hi, Daddy," she coos, planting a kiss on his cheek.

Daddy? He has a daughter?

He reaches around to take a handful of her ass, and she squeaks then giggles. "You're so naughty, Daddy."

An involuntary shudder runs through me. Nope. Not a daughter. At least, I hope not.

"Mindy, this is Blake Ramirez and Emma Jones." He points his cigar at each of us.

"Oh my gawd!" she squeals. "You're her!" She unlatches herself from him and grabs hold of my hands, pulling me away from Blake. "You're like, my idol or something."

I quirk a brow at him and mouth, 'or something'?

"You for sure should've won that award," she gushes, placing a hand to her chest, and if I'm not mistaken, a tear comes to her eye. "What they did to you..." She fans her face. "It was like, so not cool."

"Ah, thanks." I pull my hand from her grasp, waving it through the air. "It's ancient history, I'm over it."

Mindy sighs, stroking a hand down my face. "You are so brave." Then she turns to Tony. "Isn't she brave, Daddy?" He nods and she turns back to me. "I don't think I coulda showed my face anywhere after that. But here you are." She beams, bouncing up and down.

"Here I am." I hold my arms out to the side. "In the flesh."

Blake lifts a glass to his lips, but I don't miss the smirk he's sporting.

Mindy fishes around in her bra, pulling out a phone. "Can I like, get a selfie with you?" Before I can even respond she has me in a vise-like grip, her arm extended out in front with the screen facing us. She does the obligatory duck face pout while I cringe inwardly.

Once she's clicked off a few dozen shots, she scrolls through them, laughing and holding it out for me to see.

"This one is going straight to my feed." She squeals again. "My friends aren't gonna believe it!"

"Emma, we should..." Blake nods his head towards the other room, finally coming to my rescue.

"Right, of course. It was lovely to meet you, Mindy." I smile, hoping that will be the end of it, but she grabs me, pulling me into her chest.

"Oh my gawd, you too!" She leans back, her lips forming an O shape. "Oh em gee, we should totes do lunch or whatever."

"Um, yeah, maybe." Blake snickers beside me, and I shove an elbow into his side. "Have your people call my people."

I can still hear her squawking at Tony as we walk away. Pinching the bridge of my nose, I say under my breath, "God, that was painful."

"Like for sure." Blake grips my arm, mimicking her accent perfectly.

I roll my eyes, slapping a hand to his chest. "Oh my gawd, stahp."

He throws his head back, laughing. "Can you imagine what they're like in the bedroom?"

"Oh god, don't. I think I just threw up a little in my mouth."

He leans in and whispers, "Daddy."

"Eww! No, just no." I shake my head. "That conjures up all sorts of images that shouldn't exist."

"Like you've never had any daddy fantasies." He waggles his eyebrows, and neither of us can keep a straight face.

We mingle with the crowds, indulging in more champagne as we do. Every now and then I hear the shrill sound of Mindy's excitable voice over the low burble, and every time I cringe. Don't get me wrong, I love my fans, but there's something about a grown woman calling a man Daddy that gives me the heebie jeebies.

I've managed to avoid the bathrooms for most of the night so as not to be cornered with her again, but the seal is well and truly ready to burst. Excusing myself from our conversation, I stumble through the house on wobbly legs. Perhaps one too many champers to be walking around unescorted.

I find a vacant bathroom on the second floor, and after relieving myself, I fling the door open and come face to face with a man in a suit. "Oh!" I stumble backwards, giggling. "Sorry, I couldn't find the facilities downstairs. I hope that's okay." I straighten my dress and move to step around him, but he blocks me. "Excuse me," I say, pointing down the stairs. "I have to get back."

"I'm sure you do, Emma." He shoves his hands in his pockets, not moving out of my way. There's a familiar look to his face, but I can't quite place it.

"Do I know you?"

"We've met in passing." He looks me up and down with a sneer. "It's always the same."

"I'm sorry, I don't follow."

He shakes his head. "Your label might think it's cute, but addiction is addiction, no matter how you look at it."

My cheeks heat. How dare he speak to me this way. "I'm sorry, who did you say you are?"

"I didn't. I thought you'd recognize me, actually. Never mind. You'll soon know when I show the world what a selfish drunk you are." He braces his hands against the door frame, leaning in to me. "Your sister deserved better."

I rear back as if he struck me, bile rising to my throat. "I... I..."

"You what? Gonna spurt some other bullshit excuse?" He holds his arms out, looking side to side. "Where's your agent coming to your rescue now, huh?"

"I... I don't..." I shake my head as tears stream down my face. Lifting my eyes to meet his, I ask, "Who are you?"

"You really don't remember me?" He shakes his head. "I always knew you were self-absorbed."

"Who. Are. You?" I demand, poking a finger at his chest. "And how do you know about my sister?"

His eyes pin me with a look of pure hatred. "I was there."

Chapter thirty-three

"No." I shake my head. "No, I would remember if you were there."

"That's the thing about alcohol, Emma. It has a tendency to make you forget, like you forgot about Sarah."

"No." I stumble back against the basin, my palms slamming into my forehead. "No, you're lying."

"Am I?" He rakes his hand through his hair. "I had to leave early because we had family visiting. You said you would look after her."

My head jerks up, and I frown. "Joshua?"

He slow claps. "And she finally gets it."

"But you..."

"Look different? Yeah, contacts and losing forty pounds will do that."

I stare at him, still not comprehending what's going on. "What do you want from me? If it's money, I can get it for you."

He scoffs. "Your money won't bring her back!"

"You think I don't know that? Why do you think I drink? Because it's fun?" I laugh humorlessly. "I drink to forget. I drink because it hurts too damn much."

"You think this is what she would've wanted for you? She fucking idolised you, Emma, and you're shitting all over her memory." He paces back and forth. "I thought when you came here you'd honor her memory, but I'm done waiting for that to happen."

I jut my chin out, my hands on my hips. "Everything I've done is for her."

"Everything you've done? Getting off your face and embarrassing yourself in front of millions was for her? Drinking yourself into oblivion every chance you get is for her?" He stops in front of me, gripping my wrists. "You don't fool me, Emma. You're doing this for yourself, not her. That's why I'm stepping in. I'm doing this for her."

"Telling the world she was an alcoholic and I'm following in her footsteps is for her, is it?" I narrow my eyes, seething. "Sounds to me like it's to get you the kudos you're obviously reaching for, and you don't have the balls to go out there and do some real journalistic work and earn it on your own merit." I push my way past him, turning for one last jab. "I know you're angry, I'm angry too, but you don't need to drag her name through the mud to hurt me. I'm already hurting more than you could possibly know."

***

Angry tears stream down my face as I wrench the car door open and collapse into a heap on the driver's seat. I don't bother with my seatbelt, I just turn the key in the ignition and plant my foot on the accelerator. All I want to do is go home and cry myself to sleep. I should've known coming out tonight was a recipe for disaster. It's why I always make up some excuse to stay in on this date every year.

How dare he? How dare he sully my sister's memory by outing her to the world, and for what? For revenge? To prove I'm not perfect? Like I didn't already know that.

I shake my head, swiping the tears that won't stop from my face, and almost miss the corner. Pulling the wheel sharply, I swerve across the center line, not seeing the oncoming lights until it's too late. I try to correct myself, but it's no use, they're too close. Slamming my foot on the break to ease the impact, I bring my arms up to shield my face as the sound of screeching tires and crunching metal reverberates in my ears. My head bounces off the steering wheel, stunning me, and as I close my eyes, all I can hear is crying.

Chapter thirty-four

I stare up at the house, willing myself to go inside. To face Brock and tell him what I did. My heart pounds in my chest, and fresh tears spring to my eyes. I know I have to do this, but I can't get myself to move.

Cybil managed to convince the police to let me go on the proviso I don't skip the country before my hearing. She can perform miracles that woman, even though I know I don't deserve such a courtesy. She was silent on the trip to the hospital, and she didn't say much as she dropped me home either, just looked at me with disapproval. It's a look I'm going to have to get used to after this. I've gone and given Joshua even more ammo to sling at me, and I know it'll be all over the papers come morning.

Taking a deep breath, I force my feet to move up the steps and through the front door. The house is quiet, and I know Brock will have already gone to bed. The cowardly part of me hopes he doesn't wake, so I can pretend for a little bit longer.

I trudge down to the bedroom and lie on top of the sheets, careful not to disturb him. But luck is not on my side, it would seem.

He rolls towards me, but I turn away, curling in on myself as gut-wrenching sobs wrack my body. I've tried so hard to be strong, but I just can't anymore. All my pain and grief from the past four years has become an all-consuming agony like no other.

"Emma? Baby, what's wrong? Talk to me." Brock's strong arms wrap around me like a cocoon.

"I... can't...." My chest constricts, and I gulp for air. "You'll... hate... me."

"I could never hate you."

"You don't know that." I shake my head, wrapping my arms around my waist as far as they can reach.

Brock sighs, his head falling to the back of my shoulder. "Please?"

If I tell him what happened, he's going to leave and never come back. I know, because it's exactly what I'd do in his position. But if I don't tell him, I risk losing him too. It's not fair to keep stringing him along like this. He needs to know the kind of person I am.

I take a deep breath, my body shuddering as I let it out. "I crashed the car," I whisper.

"You crashed the...? Are you okay?" He spins me to look at him, his eyes raking over my body for signs of injury. I hear the intake of breath as he takes in my mangled state. My nose is broken, and bruising is already starting to appear around my eyes.

I can't bear the look of sympathy in his eyes. It's a look I don't deserve. Forcing myself to meet his gaze, I push him back to give myself the space I need. I can't have him touching me when I break his heart.

"Emma, what is it?"

"I was drinking." The words leave an acrid taste in my mouth, but I swallow it down.

He rears back as if I've slapped him, and a range of emotions cross his face. "Please tell me you're joking."

I shake my head, tears pooling in my eyes. "I wish I was." I reach for him even though I don't deserve his caress. "I'm so sorry, Brock. I wasn't thinking."

"No, you were. You were just thinking of yourself, like always."

I blanch. Does he really think that of me? Not more than three hours ago, Joshua said the same thing. Are they right? *Am* I selfish? "You don't really mean that, do you?"

He rakes his hand through his hair. "I don't know anymore." Scrubbing a hand down his face, he turns to me again. "You realize you could've killed someone? And then what?" His eyes widen and he covers his mouth with his hand. "Oh my god, you didn't, did you?"

I swallow back the lump in my throat, shaking my head profusely. "No, I swear. No one was killed." I avert my eyes, knowing what's coming next.

"Did you hurt anyone?" His voice is so quiet and calm, and it scares me. I want so much to turn back time and make it all right again. I want to go back to the ranch, where everything was so perfect.

"Emma?"

I nod, shrinking into myself.

"How bad?"

I repeat what the paramedic told me. "A broken rib and lacerations to the face."

"Jesus." He pulls even further away from me, sliding to the edge of the bed and planting his feet on the ground. Bracing his elbows on his thighs, he rests his head in his hands. "You're lucky it wasn't worse."

"I know."

The silence stretches out between us. I don't know what I can say to make this better. I don't know if we can come back from this.

"What's really going on?"

That gets my attention. "W-what?" I sniffle, rolling to face him. "What do you mean?"

"I'm not an idiot. You've been drinking even more lately, and you shut down whenever I bring it up. What aren't you telling me?"

"Nothing," I lie, shaking my head.

He sighs, looking to the ceiling. "I can't keep doing this, Emma. I thought I could, but... This isn't going to work."

Even though I expected it, panic sets in. "What do you mean? I-I thought you understood." My voice cracks as my heart breaks in two.

He stands, pacing the floor with an abruptness I've never seen before, and it's because of me. I've done this to him. I'm responsible for that look on his face.

"Understood what? You won't tell me anything! I'm sorry, Emma, but there's only so much understanding a man can have when he's watching the woman he loves fall apart before his eyes."

I blink, forcing myself to rise onto my knees. "You love me?"

He rakes a hand through his hair with a laugh, only this one isn't filled with that humor I adore. "That's what you got out of that? Of course I love you. I love you so damn much it hurts, but I can't stand by and watch you destroy yourself. I just can't."

"What are you saying? Are you... breaking up with me?"

"I'm saying I thought I could handle it—the alcohol, the secrets—but I can't. Not after this. Not anymore. Not if you refuse to let me in. And now that your drinking has hurt someone?" He shakes his head. "I don't know, maybe we need to have a break." His eyes widen and he stumbles back, seemingly shocked by his own admission.

My mouth opens and closes but no sound comes out. My lungs feel as though they're closing in on themselves, and I gasp for breath. "Is that... really what you want?" I whisper, my legs barely holding me upright.

"Not by a long shot, Emma. But I don't know what else to do. I just know I can't do this——" he gestures between us, "——anymore. I'm sorry." He goes to step towards me then stops himself, shaking his head. "I should go."

I don't trust myself to speak without throwing myself at him, so I just nod, watching him walk out the door and out of my life. I wait until I hear the front door close before I allow myself to crumple in a heap on the bed. I honestly didn't think anything could hurt me more than the loss of my sister, but watching the man I love walk away from me is a whole new hurt I didn't know existed.

Chapter thirty-five

I don't know how long I lie there for, but as daylight streams through the drapes, I manage to pull myself up and out of bed. My body may be bruised and broken, my heart torn to tatters, but I still have a movie to make. There's no doubt in my mind they'll already know what went down last night, so there's no point in hiding.

I pour myself a liquid breakfast for the road and call a cab.

When I walk through the doors, dropping my bag and jacket on the floor, everyone stops and stares. "What? Have I got something on my face?" I snort. Only about a tub of foundation to make me look halfway decent.

"Jesus, Emma. Are you okay? What the hell happened last night?" Blake runs to me, grabbing both my shoulders.

I plaster on a smile. "I'm fiiiiiine."

He frowns, pulling me out of earshot from the rest of the cast. "You're not fiiiine. Are you drunk right now?"

I shrug him off, walking backwards towards the set. "So what if I am?" I hold my arms out, looking around the room. "Just getting into character."

"Jesus." Blake pinches the bridge of his nose before addressing me again. "I can't believe you would do this after what happened last night." He brings his palm up to his forehead. "You show up here off your face and expect what exactly? A clap on the back? You got in your car and drove while drunk." He lowers his voice. "You hurt someone, Emma."

I narrow my eyes. "I don't need you to tell me that. I was there, remember?" Turning to the room, I clap my hands. "So, where are we up to?"

Bo steps in, his hand held up to stop me going any further. "You realize how irresponsible that was? Not only could you have killed someone, you could have jeopardised everything we've been working towards. You realize there are people who are relying on you to show up and get the job done?"

"I'm here, aren't I? What's the big deal? So I've had a few drinks? I play a drunk." I shrug, swaying on my feet.

"You can't be serious." Blake stalks over to me, placing a hand on my shoulder and leaning in. "I shouldn't have to explain this to a professional." When I don't respond, he shakes his head. "Christ, Emma. Your character is a drunk, not you. You can't show up here out of your tree and expect us to carry on as if it's just another day."

"Ever heard of method acting?" Sarcasm drips from my voice as I lean back with pursed lips. I'm like a runaway train, I just can't seem to stop hurting the people I love, and the worst part is, I don't care. All I want is for him to get out of my face so I can have another drink.

"Method acting?" He laughs incredulously. "That's not how this works and you know it. Stop being facetious."

"You're being facetious," I mutter under my breath.

With a sigh, he steps in close, his eyes searching mine. "Come on, Emma. This isn't you."

"Pfft. Like you didn't know what you were getting yourself into when you asked me to audition. You saw the Oscars. You know what I am." I point my finger at his chest accusingly.

He swipes a hand through his hair in frustration. "I thought that was a goddamn publicity stunt! I didn't realize you had a problem. If I did, I never would've given you the role." He pauses, looking to Bo and Javier before meeting my eyes again. "You *do* have a problem, Emma. You need to get help."

I blink. "So, what? You're firing me? Because I had a drink before coming to work?"

He takes my hands, ducking his head until I look him in the eye. "I can't have you on set like this. We can't risk our reputation on this, we're not big enough. We'll lose our backing. I'm sorry."

I know I can't be hearing him right, because there's no way the Blake I know would send me packing right when I need a friend the most. I know I'm being a jerk to him, but friends are meant to see through that. "You're seriously firing me?" Tears pool and spill down my cheeks as I take a step back. Swiping a hand across my cheeks, I whisper, "I thought we were friends."

"We are friends, Emma. That's exactly why I'm doing this. You need to get help before you get yourself in trouble."

"I don't need some shrink to tell me alcohol is the devil. I could give it up like that." I attempt to click my fingers to punctuate my point, but no sound comes out. "Damn it," I hiss under my breath. "You know what I mean."

Gathering my bag and jacket, I stride to the exit, pausing in the doorway. "Oh, and this." I wave a hand between Blake and I. "This isn't going to work. We should see other people." I make a point of looking at Javier before I storm out the door.

***

"Well, well. Fancy seeing you here."

"What do you want, Marty?" I throw back another shot, slamming my glass on the bar. "Another."

Marty slides into the seat next to me. "You might want to slow down on those, sweetheart."

"Yeah? Well you might want to keep your nose in your own business."

He whistles low. "Word on the street is you're seeing my boy. I think that makes it my business, don't you?"

"You, of all people, should know you can't believe everything you hear." I look at him pointedly.

He chuckles. "Too true. You saying it ain't so?"

"I'm saying it's not something I wanna talk about." The bartender hands me another shot of vodka and I slug it back.

"I've got this one." He tosses a few bucks on the bar, holding up two fingers. "One for me and another for the lady."

"I don't need your charity. I can buy my own drinks."

"Forgive me for saying, but I hear you're... between jobs at the minute."

I snort, shaking my head. "Word sure travels fast."

"You forget, sweetheart, I have eyes and ears all over this town. No one so much as sneezes without my knowing about it."

"That so?"

He nods, lighting a cigarette and taking a drag. He offers the pack to me.

"That shit'll send you to an early grave." I tip my head back, downing another shot, the irony of my words not lost on me.

Marty chuckles again. "I could say the same thing, sweetheart."

I slam my glass down, spinning in my seat to face him. "We gonna just sit here shooting the breeze, or are you gonna tell me what you want?"

"I like you. You're a fiery one." He puts his cigarette pack back in his pocket. "I'm gonna level with ya. I have my finger in a lot of pies, as any good businessman does. This here bar is one of mine, in fact." He raises his glass in salute to the bartender. "I like to know all that's going on in here, and there's been a bit of bad press following you, and that includes when you was here with my boy."

"Right. Is this the part where you kick me out too? Might as well, right? Everyone else is doing it." I tap the bar. "One more for the road."

"I'm not asking you to leave. Just letting you know I'm keeping tabs." He backs away, puffing a smoke ring from his mouth. "Purely business, you understand."

My mouth goes dry as I watch him leave, his thinly veiled threat hanging in the air.

Chapter thirty-six

My head pounds in a steady rhythm. I peel my eyes open and blink against the fluorescent light of the bathroom. The cool tiles beneath me offer no relief as I drag myself to my feet. I've got one shoe on, and my pants are down by my ankles. There's vomit down the side of the toilet, and I realize I must've passed out on the floor.

"Oh god," I mutter as I brace against the vanity. The reflection staring back at me is one on death's door. The bruising has darkened, and my eyes are bloodshot. I could give Beetlejuice a run for his money. I snort, laughing at my sorry state of affairs until it morphs into an all-out bawl. I have royally screwed up. I've lost everything good in my life.

Sliding to the floor, I rest my head in my hands and let the tears fall. Tears for Sarah, and tears for myself. All this time I thought I was doing it for her, but somewhere along the way, I started doing things for myself too. I loved my job with Blake and Bo, and more than that, I loved my life with Brock. And I threw it all away. Poof. Just like that.

The pounding continues until I realize it's coming from the front of the house. Someone is knocking at the door.

"Go away!" I cry through my tears. "Just leave me alone."

"Emma?" My head snaps up at the sound of his voice. "Emma, I just want to talk. Please, will you let me in?"

I scramble to my feet, pulling my pants up on the way.

"Brock?" I pinch my arm to see if it's real.

"Yes, it's me."

With my heart pounding, I unlock the door and step aside. "What do you want?" I whisper.

"Please, Emma." He takes my hands. "I've been thinking about it, and I can't just throw it all away, not without giving it one last shot." He brushes a hair behind my ear, and I can't help but let my cheek fall into his hand. Tears fill his eyes as he strokes his thumb against my skin. "Please, I know I said I wouldn't push, but I need to know what's going on with you."

I close my eyes, sighing. "You can read all about it in the paper."

"I don't want to read about it, I want to hear it from you."

"I..." What's the point in hiding anymore? He'll find out sooner or later, it may as well come from me. "Okay," I whisper, turning and walking into the kitchen.

I go about the motions, making coffee, trying to work up the nerve to speak.

I place our cups between us, then stare at my hands. They're shaking. One tear falls, slowly sliding down the side as I close my eyes and take a breath.

"Sarah was my kid sister. She died four years ago, on April the third. Those first few weeks after her death, I could barely drag myself out of bed to face the day. I know it sounds cliché, but I saw her face everywhere I looked; in the sun as it tried to rouse me from my sleep, in the glow of the moon as it kissed me goodnight, and in my mother's eyes as she looked at me with sorrow." I shake my head, a sad smile on my face. "Sarah had been a miniature version of her, more so than me, but with a personality ten times the size.

Losing her was like losing a part of myself, and I guess it had to be even harder for my parents, but I couldn't see it at the time. All I saw was their blame, and at the same time, the worry that they were losing me too."

"Emma." Brock sweeps a hair from my face. "I'm sure they didn't blame you."

I shake my head. "No, they did. I get it. I blame me too." He tries to speak but I hold my hand up, continuing. "She was only 16, and I was the 'cool big sister'. My friends were older, and we partied, a lot. She was just a kid, but she wanted to tag along with me, so I let her. At first it was just a drink or two, but it didn't take long before she was getting trolleyed with the rest of us. She was underage, so I bought her alcohol every time we went out. It was meant to be harmless fun, and it was, at first." I pause, needing to take a breath before I can carry on, knowing my heart is about to rip in two.

"I tried telling myself it was normal for someone her age to drink as much as she was. I didn't want to believe it was anything more than that, but it was. She had an addiction, and I encouraged it. Great big sister, huh?" I laugh humorlessly.

"The night she died, we'd had a blinder of a night, and she'd been hitting the booze hard. I'd tried to get her to drink water between drinks, but I don't think she listened, and I was too busy having my own fun. It was mine and Bradley's six-month anniversary, so we'd invited a few friends around to his flat, and things just got out of hand.

"Sarah had asked me to buy her absinthe. I knew it was too strong for her, but I bought it anyway. I just wanted her to be happy. I guess I forgot how happy and full of life she was without alcohol." I frown. "How could I forget that?"

Brock takes my hand. "What happened?"

"She passed out. I had to get Bradley to help me carry her to the spare bedroom to sleep it off. It never occurred to me to check on her through the night. What kind of person leaves her sister comatose and alone?"

I swipe a tear from my face. "Asphyxiation, that's what they called it. In her comatose state, she wasn't with it enough to roll over when she threw up. She just lay there, choking in her sleep while I was in the other room, partying. She died all alone. My beautiful, life-of-the-party sister had her light extinguished because I was too selfish to check on her, and I have to live with that, Brock. Every damn day I have to live with that."

"Emma." There's pity in his voice and I can't stand it. I don't deserve his pity. "It wasn't your fault."

"Don't. I did this. Me. I'm the one responsible for her death, and I know it." I stand, walking to the door. "You were right to leave. I'm poison. I hurt the people I care most about."

"Emma, don't do this. Please, just talk to me."

"I tried, Brock. I tried so damn hard to be what you want me to be, but it's exhausting. I can't keep pretending I'm okay."

"I'm not asking you to be okay, I'm asking you to let me in, to let me help." He strides over, taking my hands again. "We can get through this together. Just let me help you."

I pull my hands away, twisting my lips to the side. "You wanna help? Get me a bottle of vodka and help me forget."

His face drops. "I can't do that, Emma. That's not how we get past this."

Folding my arms across my chest, I jut my chin out. "Well, that's how *I* get past this. I'll be drinking with or without you, so either you join me, or you go and leave me to it."

Chapter thirty-seven

"Hit me with another." I tap the bar. "And keep them coming."

The bartender throws his tea-towel over his shoulder before grabbing the bottle of vodka from the back shelf. He pours a single, but when I raise my brows at him, he quickly adds more.

I hold my glass in the air, nodding my head towards him before taking a large mouthful. The cool liquid slides down my throat, instantly warming my insides. I keep going over my conversation with Brock, wondering if I did the right thing. All he wanted to do was help me, and I turned him away.

"This seat taken?"

I wave my hand to my side. "It's a free country."

"That it is." His hand lands on my thigh, and I glance down with a frown. "Scotch on the rocks, and whatever she's drinking."

"Where's *Mindy* this evening?" I remove his hand from me, placing it on his own lap.

He chuckles. "Come on. What's a little friendly touching between friends?"

I snort, shaking my head. "You sure have a weird idea of what friends are." Tapping the bar again, I lift two fingers. "Make it a double."

"So it's true then?"

I swivel in my chair, one brow raised in question. "What's true?"

"You and Blake. I hear you're no longer together. Both on and off the screen." He shakes his head with a tsk. "That's a damn shame."

"It is what it is. No use crying over it. There'll be other jobs." I sniff, turning back to the bar. "You know what? Just leave me the bottle. That'll save us some time." I throw a wad of cash on the bar. "That cover it?"

The bartender flicks through the notes, then slides the bottle across the bar with a curt nod.

Lifting the bottle, I fill my glass to the brim, then hold it over Tony's glass. "You joining me, *friend*?"

He tilts his glass. "What the hell, eh? Can't leave a pretty little thing like you to drink by herself." His hand lands on my thigh again, and like before, I pick it up and push it away.

I level him with a stare. "You wanna drink with me, fine. But I'm not out for anything else, okay? I'm not interested."

He raises his hands, palms out. "Fair call. I'll be on my best behavior. Promise." Lifting his glass to his lips, he pauses. "It's just... I can help you, you know?"

I bet you could.

"Help me how exactly?"

"I know a lot of people in the industry, you must know that." He glances out the side of his eye as he tosses his drink back.

"And?"

"And, I could put in a good word, get things moving again. Being seen with me would do wonders for your career." He leans in, whispering, "I can talk anyone into anything. Just say the word, and they'll be eating out of the palm of your hand."

I tilt my head, pursing my lips. "Right. And what do you get out of it?" I'm not stupid enough to think offers like that don't come without strings.

With a grin like the Cheshire cat, he leans in, whispering, "I'm sure we could think of something." He squeezes my thigh, throwing a wink my way. "I can be a real accommodating guy. How do you think Mindy got that modelling contract?" His thumb draws circles on my leg, and my skin crawls.

"Hard work and determination?" I deadpan, pouring another hefty glass of vodka and tipping it back.

Tony barks out a laugh, his hand slamming down on the bar. "Mindy? Hard work and determination? Ha!" Holding his glass out towards me, he points. "You've got a smart mouth on you. I like it." His tongue darts out to wet his lips. "I imagine that mouth could get you into all kinds of trouble." His hooded gaze sears into me as he leans forward, his hand slowly sliding further up my thigh.

Bile rises to my throat at his insinuation. "Look, Tony, I appreciate it, but like I said, I'm not interested." Spinning back to the bar, I swipe the bottle and grab my purse. "I might just take this home."

"Come now. Don't be so dramatic." He sneers, leaning in close. "I can wait."

My eyes travel from his beady eyes to the obvious bulge in his pants, and I shudder. He'll be waiting until my body is dead and buried before that situation ever happens.

"You'll be waiting a long time. I'm not in the habit of taking other women's seconds, and I just came out of a relationship. I'm sure you understand." Draping my jacket over my arm, I slide off the stool to leave, but he stops me with a hand to my wrist.

"Don't go. Mindy left me." There's an almost human quality to his eyes this time, and maybe it's the alcohol taking hold, but I feel sorry for him in this moment. "I could really use a friend right now."

"Just friends?"

"Just friends."

***

"I shouldgo." The clock on the wall is too fuzzy for me to make out the numbers, but it must be well after midnight. Between the two of us, we've downed a bottle of vodka and one of scotch, and I'm not feeling so good right now. I swivel my head side to side, searching for my jacket and purse.

"Here." Tony hands them to me, a smile across his face. "Let me call you a cab."

"Noooo." I swipe a hand through the air as I try to stand. "I'll be fiiiiine."

"It's the least I can do after you let me talk your ear off all night." Maybe he's not so bad after all.

"I..." I look around the room with a frown. "What wassss I saying?"

He chuckles. "That you're going to let me take you home."

"Ohhh, thas right." I nod, waving a finger at him. "Sucha gentleman." My eyes close as I let my head fall back.

"Whoa there." His arms wrap around me, holding me up. "I've got you. I'll take real good care of you."

***

Where the hell am I? The last thing I remember, Tony was taking me home. But this doesn't look like any room in my house. I raise up onto my elbows, peering around the room. There's something vaguely familiar about the place, but for the life of me, I can't remember.

"Ah, good. You're awake." Tony stalks towards me with two drinks in his hand. He holds one out to me, and I take it with a frown.

"Where are we?"

"My place, of course." He grins, trailing a finger down my cheek and neck then to my breast.

"I don't understand. You were taking me home."

"Yes. My home." He waves his hand in an arc. "You don't remember what you promised me?"

My eyes follow his hand. There's a camera set up in the corner of the room, and my clothes are draped across a chair next to it. My heart pounds in my chest as I drop my gaze to see I'm lying on a large bed in only my underwear.

"W-what's going on?" I ask, scooting myself to the far side of the bed. "Why am I not wearing any clothes?" Please dear god; tell me I didn't have sex with him. I try to focus on my body and how it feels. My heart is racing and my stomach is roiling, but I don't feel anything else.

Tony eases onto the bed, his sweaty hand landing on my ankle. "For the show, of course." His grip tightens and he yanks me towards him. The glass I was holding flies out of my hand, vodka splattering into my face.

"I don't want this... Please, Tony. I don't know what I promised, but I've changed my mind." I kick out with my other leg, but he grabs hold of that one too. "Please," I plead. "Let me go. I won't say anything, I swear."

Pinning my body underneath his, he strokes a hand down my hair. "Shhh, just close your eyes and enjoy it." He licks his lips. "I know I will."

"Please... don't do this." Tears spill down my cheeks and onto the bed. "I don't want this."

The hand stroking my hair rears back and he strikes me across the face. "Shut up!" he snarls. His tongue drags across his lip, and then he's leaning towards me. His hot breath mingles with my own, and then his lips crush onto mine, his tongue forcing its way inside. One hand snakes up between us, ripping the delicate fabric of my bra, exposing me. "Yes," he moans, pinning my hands above me as he lowers his mouth to my breast. A sharp sting resonates through my body as he clamps his teeth around my nipple.

I cry out in pain, but it only spurs him on. "Yes, that's it."

His face is covered with sweat, his beady eyes devouring my body as they did the first time we met. I squeeze my eyes shut, not wanting to believe what's happening to me. *It's just a dream. It's just a dream. It's just a dream.*

But it's not. It's my worst nightmare, and I can't wake up.

"Please stop," I plead. My head lolls to the side as I stare vacantly at the red flashing light on the camera. This sick bastard is going to get off watching me beg, and something tells me this isn't the first time he's done it either. There are probably other girls out there who have been taken advantage of by this man who thinks he has the right to our bodies.

I can't let him do it. Not to me, and not to anyone ever again.

With a sudden surge of anger, I buck my hips and push against his hand with all my might. He smirks as if it's all just a game. "Do it again."

So I do, only this time I bring my knee up as hard as I can. He gasps, his body tensing up as he rolls to the side. "Bitch!"

I don't waste any time, my body moving on autopilot as I race to grab my clothes. I'm halfway out the door when I remember the camera. With a quick glance to the bed to make sure he's still there, I turn back. The thing is attached to a tripod, and I can't figure out how to remove it, but I don't have time to muck around. Tony is grunting, but on his feet already.

"Get back here, you stupid bitch!" he roars, one hand cradling his less-than-impressive manhood, while he storms towards me.

Swinging the tripod up into the air, I wield it, holding him off. "Get away from me!"

There's a loud bang from somewhere else in the house, and I turn wide eyes to him. "You sick fuck! You've got someone else tied up here, haven't you?"

His eyes dart to the door and back to me, confusion mixing with his anger. Realization dawns. He has no idea who is in the house.

"In here!" I scream as loud as I can. "I'm in here! Please help!"

"Shut up!" he seethes, making a grab for the tripod.

"Emma!"

"Brock! I'm in here!" I bang my hand against the wall behind me, the tripod dropping slightly. Tony lunges forward, yanking it from my hands and tossing it across the room. Before I can comprehend what's happening, I'm forced against the wall, his body pressed to mine. He covers my mouth with his hand, bringing a finger to his lips. "Shhhh."

Footsteps thud down the hall outside, along with the sound of doors opening and closing. "Emma!"

It all happens so quickly. The door flies open, and Tony's body suddenly flies across the room. Two large men I've never seen before loom over him, their thick legs pinning him to the ground.

"Where is she?" Brock's panicked voice finds my ears, and I try to turn my head to search for him, but he's already there, scooping me into his arms. "Oh god, Emma. Are you okay? Did he hurt you?" His tears mingle with my own as I sob both from relief and shame.

Over his shoulder, I see Blake saying something to the two men before they haul Tony to his feet and march him out.

"Emma?" Brock pulls back, his eyes raking over me. "Are you hurt?"

I shake my head, unable to find the words. Blake bends down, grabbing my top and handing it to me. "Here," he says gently.

"How did you know?" I ask. "How did you know I needed you?"

Blake runs a hand through his hair. "Dad. He had his men watching you." He sighs. "I can't even be mad at him because if he hadn't..." His voice trails off. "When they saw Tony carry you out of the bar, they contacted me. Thought I'd want to know what my girl was up to." He pauses, meeting my gaze. "I knew you'd never go willingly with him."

I shake my head vehemently. "I don't even remember getting in the car." My voice is quiet, filled with regret. "I was drunk."

"Shh, we don't have to go over that now." Brock cups my face in his hands, resting his forehead against mine. "All that matters is you're safe."

"He filmed it," I whisper, nodding my head at the camera on the floor. "He probably has others too." I turn to Blake. "Mindy." My voice cracks.

"I'll have the boys do a sweep of the house once they're finished with him."

I nod my head in thanks.

"I'm so sorry I wasn't there, Emma. If I'd just stayed with you..."

I place a finger across his lips. "Don't. It's not your fault. I shouldn't have been at the bar." I swallow thickly, meeting his gaze. "You were right." I look to Blake. "You all were." Brock goes to speak but I stop him. "I didn't want to admit it before, but I can't pretend anymore. I have a problem." I smile through my tears. "I'm sorry it took me so long to realize."

"You don't have to apologize for anything."

"No, I do." I shake my head. "I put you through hell when all I really needed to do was reach out and accept your help." I laugh humorlessly. "I just wish it didn't take the grubby hands of a sleazeball to make me see the light." Closing my eyes, I take a deep breath. "I'm ready to do this. I want to get better." Flicking my eyes between the two of them, I ask, "Will you help me?"

Epilogue

Ten months later

"I think that's everything we need." Sydney stands, brushing her hands down her pencil skirt and tucking her notebook in her bag. She turns to Cybil. "I'll have a draft copy sent straight to your office in the next day or so. Any discrepancies, just sing out."

Cybil offers her hand. "I appreciate that, Miss Marshall."

"Let me walk you out." I clasp my hands in front of me as I walk to the door. I find holding something, even just my own hand, can stop me reaching for a drink.

Stepping out into the crisp air, I turn to her, taking both her hands in mine. "Thank you for doing this."

"Thank you. What you're doing, speaking out against a man like Tony Bradford? It's a gamechanger. You're doing the right thing."

"I had to start sometime, right?" I laugh.

She smiles, giving my hand a squeeze. "Laying all your flaws out there for everyone to see and showing how you came back from it—I don't think you realize how much of an inspiration you're going to be for other women out there. I think this could be the start of something bigger than both of us."

I nod. "I hope so. Even if it only reaches one person and helps them to speak out, then I've done what I set out to do. I'm not hiding who I am anymore."

Her eyes fill with tears. "Believe me, you've already reached someone."

"Sydney." I pull her into my arms, stroking a hand down her hair. "If I can do it, you can do it. Okay?" I pull back. "Don't let the bastard win."

She huffs out a laugh, swiping a hand across her eyes. "Oh, I won't." She walks down the steps and over to her car. Pausing at the door, she says, "Good luck for tonight."

I grin, waving as she pulls down the drive.

Brock's arms wrap around me from behind. "How're you feeling?"

I lean back, inhaling his masculine scent. "I think it went well, don't you?"

"Mmm, but that's not what I was talking about." He spins me to face him, his hands automatically circling my hips as he plants a kiss to my nose.

"Oh, you mean the Oscars?" I wave a hand through the air. "I'm fine."

"Not even a little nervous?"

I bring my hands around to cup his cheeks. "Nope." I grin. "Should I be?"

A throat clears behind us. "Don't you two have somewhere to be?" Cybil stands with her arms folded across her chest and her toe tapping against the ground. Her glasses have slipped down her nose, and if I'm not mistaken, there's a hint of wetness on her lashes.

"Aww, Cybil." I open my arms and step towards her.

"No." She holds her hand up in the air. "Don't you dare."

"Sorry, the hug train has already left the station and it can't stop until it gets a hug."

"That doesn't even make sense." She turns her eyes to Brock. "Make her stop."

He holds his hands up. "Sorry, no can do. I'm not getting in the middle of whatever this is."

"No point fighting it, Cybil." I stop in front of her, raising my brow to ask for permission.

She sighs, rolling her eyes so far she can probably see the door behind her. "Fine." She holds her arms out, and I crush her to me.

"Don't worry, I won't tell Dawn how much of a softy you are." I grin, pulling back. "I'll see you soon, okay?"

She nods, pushing her glasses back up on her face. "Shall I send a car?"

"Don't be silly. Betsy mark II will get us there."

"Of course. How could I forget that hideous thing?" She stalks down the steps.

"Don't be hating on her because she's beautiful. Tell you what, I'm sure we could find you a matching one."

"I think I'll be fine. Don't be late."

"Would I be late to my own party?" I ask innocently.

"You'd be late to your own funeral," she quips.

My jaw drops. "Did you just crack a joke?" I turn to Brock, draping my arms across his shoulder. "Our little girl is growing up."

***

Cameras flash as we walk down the red carpet. Brock on one arm, and Blake on the other. We stop and pose, smiling for the cameras, while reporters call my name. It's a rush like no other, and one I don't think I'll ever get used to.

We step into the ballroom, the tables laden with alcohol and goodie bags. Brock swipes the bottle from our table and hands it to a passing waiter. "None for us, thanks."

The atmosphere is almost electric as Hollywood's finest mix and mingle. In contrast to my last appearance here, I sit quietly, observing my peers. I feel like I missed out on so much in my drink-addled haze over the past few years. So many amazing people here, and I chose to drink my days away instead of getting to know them.

The lights dim and the music starts.

I cheer as the awards are announced for each category, gleefully clapping until my hands hurt.

When the award for Best Actress is about to be announced, Blake takes my hand. "This is it."

My name is listed alongside a number of brilliant actresses, each one deserving in their own right. The camera pans over each of us, waiting for the name to be announced.

"And the winner is.... Emma Jones for her role as Taylor in *Taylor's Mistake!*"

I look around at all the smiling faces, not quite believing my ears. "Did they just say my name?"

Blake laughs. "They did."

"Really?" He nods, pulling me to my feet. I wrap him in a hug, squeezing tight, before grabbing Brock and dragging him up on stage with me.

"I, um. Wow." The crowd laughs. "I had to check for a minute there that I heard it right this time. Don't want a repeat of last year." I clutch the Oscar to my chest and peer around behind me, making the audience laugh again. "Seriously though. This has been one hell of a year. As many of you know, I've made a few changes." I hold up my sobriety chip. "Ten months sober and counting." Everyone cheers. "Anyway, I want to thank Blake and Bo for taking a chance on me, and for hanging around while I got my shit together. I'll never forget what you did for me." My voice breaks as I meet his gaze across the room. "And my agent, Cybil, and PR, Dawn. You guys stood by me when no one else did. I owe you so much."

"I take cash and check!" Dawn hollers from the back, and I can't help but laugh.

"And of course, my fiancé, Brock." I squeeze his hand. "Thank you for standing by me when I didn't deserve it and helping me realize I deserve to be happy." I smile, wiping the tears from my face. "Which is why this will be the last appearance I make for a while."

There's an audible intake of breath through the audience, followed by murmuring.

"That's right, folks. My cowboy has turned me country." I lean down, gripping the hem of my dress and pulling it forward like a stripper does his pants. Underneath I'm in full Ellie-May getup, with a sign that says "little critter" pointing to my belly.

A mixture of laughter and cheering fills the room as people get to their feet, clapping.

It's a surreal feeling to be in the exact same spot I was last year, but with two completely different endings. One was filled with embarrassment and shame, while the other is pure joy and hope. Hope for a wonderful future on the ranch that molded my husband-to-be into the man he is today. Hope that it'll bring the same joy to our daughter, Sarah, and any other little critters we create.

With the music signalling my time to wrap it up, I take Brock's hand in mine, hold the Oscar in the air, and address my peers one last time. "Y'all come back now, ya hear?"

A Note From the Author

Thank you so much for taking the time to read Emma! It was over a year in the making, and I'm so glad to finally bring it to you.

Hopefully you enjoyed reading it as much as I enjoyed writing it. If you did, I would love it if you could leave a review. Reviews not only help our work to be seen, they also offer valuable feedback.

Once again, thank you for reading!

Stacey xxx

Acknowledgements

First of all, I have to thank the Ashburton Writers' Group for always pushing me to step outside my comfort zone. It was one of your challenges that inspired this story! Thank you for being an inspiration, and my cheering squad. I always know you're behind me 100%.

To Launa, my US correspondent and friend. Thank you for making sure I haven't made my American characters speak in weird kiwi tongue. You rock!

To Trina, my amazing friend who pores over every single word I write and makes sure I don't sound like an idiot. Thank you for encouraging me to write all those years ago, and for continuing to support me and my dreams. Love you, chick xxx

To my family, I thank you for putting up with me shutting myself away for hours on end to write. I couldn't do this without your support.

To all the bloggers who helped to share my book with the world, I thank you. I know how hard you all work to spread the word of us authors, and believe me, it is very much appreciated. You're all fabulous!

And of course, to my readers, I thank you for taking the time to read my words. You make all the sleepless nights while ideas swirl through my mind worthwhile. It's because of you that I can do this amazing job, and it's because of you that I'll continue doing it.

About the Author

Stacey Broadbent is a multi-genre author from New Zealand. She writes under three different names and a variety of genres, so there is something to suit most tastes. You can find her LGBTQIA reads under the name Cyan Tayse, and children's books under the name Stacey Jayne.

An avid reader and lover of all things bookish, Stacey has made it her goal to share about her favourite authors and books she's read, while also building her own publishing story. She is a qualified proofreader and is embarking on a new journey of study - Library and Information Skills.

She is a member of the Unhinged Kiwi Booktalk discord group, and a great bunch of Canterbury based bookstagrammers. Her TBR is never-ending, and though she struggles to keep up with it, she continues to add more.

As well as reading, her hobbies include LEGO, cross-stitch, crochet, and diamond art, and you can often find her sharing about her latest project on TikTok.

If you feel like stalking her, here are the links!

www.staceybroadbent.com/
www.facebook.com/StaceyBroadbentAuthor
www.amazon.com/author/staceybroadbent
Goodreads: https://goo.gl/YJ6dXa
www.instagram.com/authorstaceybroadbent/
www.bookbub.com/authors/stacey-broadbent
www.tiktok.com/@authorstaceybroadbent

Other books by Stacey Broadbent

Standalone

Never Judge a Book

Emma

Deep Heat

Lady Luck: A Deep Heat bonus novella

Fever

A Christmas Tail

Broken

Awesome Applesauce

A Step in Time series

Dancing through the Storm

Dancing in Circles

Dancing with Destiny

A Step in Time: the complete series

Super Mum series
Frazzled

Frazzled and Frumpy

Frazzled, Frumpy and Fabulous!

Super Mum: the complete series

Dark sins novellas
Sins of the Flesh

Mine

Hellhounds MC
Cut Loose

Break Loose

Let Loose (coming soon)

Short Stories and Poetry
Musings, Mournings, and Misadventures

Musings, Mayhem, and Mystery

Musings, Magic, and Mischief

Musings of a Writer: the complete collection

Anthologies
Scars to your Beautiful

Witching Hour: Vices and Virtues

The White Ribbon Collection
Key to my Heart
A Touch of Inspiration
No Place Like Home
Serendipity
Lucky Star
Hellhounds